Secret Justice

Secret Justice

Wesley Nelson

iUniverse, Inc.
Bloomington

Secret Justice

iUniverse books may be ordered through booksellers or by contacting:

iUniverse
1663 Liberty Drive
Bloomington, IN 47403
www.iuniverse.com
1-800-Authors (1-800-288-4677)

ISBN: 978-1-4620-6828-9 (sc)
ISBN: 978-1-4620-6829-6 (ebk)

Printed in the United States of America

iUniverse rev. date: 03/07/2012

CHAPEL HILL. CARRBORO. HILLSBORUGH AREA.
ORANGE COUNTY N.C.

FADE IN
FICTION-DRAMA-SCREENPLAY
INT-EXT-NIGHT
APRIL-10-2005—A WARM SPRING NIGHT
SLUG-LINE-SEVEN-ELEVEN-STORE-(915'PM
(NO OTHER CUSTOMER'S IN THE STORE AT THIS TIME.)

(DIALOGUE)

A medium tall thin Caucasian vigilant dangerous drug attitude wild looking man name BRUCE HAGAN, enter the store on rosemary street in chapel hill. A Mexican employee man name GARCIA LOPEZ, stand's behind the counter, short looked over at him. (He speaks good English) BRUCE just walk's over to the potato chip's and he just open a bag of classica lay's potato chip's and started to eat them.

(GARCIA)

Sir, you need to pay before you eat. (said he, in a calm voice.) (HIS LEFT HAND OUT IN FRONT OF HIM)

(BRUCE look's at the clerk, walking toward the counter.)

(BRUCE)

This is A stick up, motherfucker, give me all of your fucking money. (PULLING HIS GUN OUT OF THE WASTE BAN OF HIS PANT'S POINTING IT AT THE CLERK, PAYING NO ATTENTION TO THE CAMER ABOVE THE CLERK'S HEAD.)

(said he in a loud angry voice)

(CONT GARCIA)

Sir, you can have the chip's, this is not necessary, please leave sir, just leave, please. (said he with a very nervously voice, surprise look on his face, shaking his head no.)

(DIALOGUE)

BRUCE, fired one shot into the clerk's chest, killing him instantly, jumped the counter, clean out all the paper money from the cash register, get cigarette and leave the scene in a white 1999 Toyota Nissan car.

SLUG-LINE-SAME SCENE (DIALOGUE)

Ten minutes later two young African American teenage girl's name TAMMY PEEK and JESSICA KELLY enter the store and found GARCIA laying against the bottom shelf on the floor dead under the tobacco behind the counter. They very quickly ran back out side in shock, using the pay phone at the corner of the store, they dial 911.

(DIALOGUE)

As uniform police officer's with forensic criminology immediately arrived on the scene. As police putting yellow crime tape around the front of the store, other people started to gathering around outside the store as well. Two of the finesse's homicide professional detective arrived on the scene as well. A medium tall African American women name MICHELLE REYNOLDS, with her partner, a medium tall Caucasian man name STEVE STEIN.

SLUG-LINE-SAME SCENE—(DIALOGUE)

REYNOLDS talk's to a forensic name HENRY, (Caucasian short) coming out of the store.

(REYNOLDS)

(sensible)

So how do it look's in there HENRY asked her?

(HENRY)

Nodded his head no, pointing his right thumb over his shoulder) That guy in there, never had a chance, he were shot at close range, and it is possible he were dead before he hit the floor, look's like with a 38 to me.

(STEIN)
sensitive
How long has it been since this shooting took place? Do we have any witness or better yet who found the body?

(HENRY)
(As he started to walk away)
Maybe 15 to 20 minutes top's when this guy was kill,
(He pointed his finger)
I think the two black girl's standing over there talking to your people, (The police) found the body and call it in

(DIALOGUE)
As REYNOLDS and STEIN enter the store a forensic name AIL (Caucasian short) were taking picture of GARCIA and the crime scene. STEIN notice the camer on the wall above he tell's REYNOLDS.

(DIALOGUE)
(REYNOLDS talk's to AIL as he look's at her.)

(REYNOLDS)
serious
AIL, what do we have here, a robbing homicide?
(pointing her finger at the camer)
AIL do you know if that camer were turn on when this crime were committed? (They both look's at the camer)

(AIL)
(look's at MICHELLE seriously)
Yes detective, this was a robbery homicide. as if that camer were turn on or not, I don't know at this time. But we will take the tape back to the lab to see if anything is on it, answer him.

(STEIN put's his right hand on AIL shoulder)

(STEIN)
serious

Good job AIL, MICHELLE, I'm going out here to have a talk with the girl's, maybe they saw something.

(CONT DIALOGUE)
STEIN walk's out the store and walked to TAMMY and JESSICA. (They both looked at him as he showed his badge.)

(STEIN)
Hi, I'm detective STEIN, can I talk to the both of you for a few minutes here?(asked he sensible polite?)
(They nodded their heads yes.)

(DIALOGUE)
(In the mean time inside the store, MICHELLE talk's to AIL)

(REYNOLDS)
AIL, do we know who this guy is?
(asked her with a sense of human?)

(AIL)
He have a wallet here.
(He take's it out of a plastic bag and open it in his hand His name is GARCIA LOPEZ, also there is a address here.
(answer he serious.) (He give's it to her, while he continue taking picture.)

(DIALOGUE)
Just as MICHELLE were looking into the wallet, a uniform police officer name ROY(Tall black fat) enter through the door. MICHELLE looked at him.

(CONT REYNOLDS)
ROY, have we started a canvas yet?
(asked her with passion?)

(ROY)
Yes we have, but we having found nothing yet.
(answer he seriously, A little irritate.)

(REYNOLDS)
Well, if and when you do, let me know first,
(nodded her head yes, said her.)

(DIALOGUE)
(ROY nodded his head yes and exit back out the store door.)
(Back out side)

(STEIN)
Can you all tell me what did you see or hear,
(asked he polite?)

(JESSICA)
When we walked in for a drink and candy, we saw that man laying on the floor, it looked like he had been shot with all that blood on the floor,
(said her very serious, a little excited.)

(STEIN)
Did you see anyone else, like someone come running out or a car leaving or someone walking down the street? (asked he?)
(He look' at TAMMY)

(TAMMY)
We were so scared we just ran out of there, when we saw that man laying in the floor. (Nodded her head no) I don't remember seeing anyone coming out or any car leaving the store. (said her still a little shaking up))

(STEIN)

(He take's two of his cards out of his wallet and give's it to them.)

If you all think of anything else, give me a call and thank you guy's for talking to me. said he)

(DIALOGUE)

As STEIN turned and walk's away toward the store, TAMMY and JESSICA headed for their home's down rosemary street in a hurry.

(In the store)

As two other forensic guys with the county coroner office, were preparing the decrease body for transporting it back to their office. REYNOLDS, AIL, and STEIN took the camer tape back to headquarters on churton street to review it.

INT-SLUG-LINE
SAME-NIGHT-NEW SCENE-HEADQUARTER'S

(CONT DIALOGUE)

They carried the tape down stair's to the computer technology room and gave it to a forensic technology name BILL. (Caucasian medium tall, big fat man.) They walked through a glass door where BILL were setting down in a chair. (He turn's around)

(AIL)

BILL, these two detective here need you to rewind this tape. It may have something on it, to do with a homicide said he with intelligent)

(He handed BILL the tape and walked out.)

(DIALOGUE)

BILL, put the tape in and rewind it, while REYNOLDS and STEIN pull's two chair's up and have a set behind him. suddenly the tape stop, and BILL played it forward slow, suddenly in walk's lieutenant of detective man name SCOTT MACK. (They all turned around and look's at him.) (Caucasian medium tall)

(SCOTT)

BILL, have you found anything on that tape yet of any interest? asked he seriously?

(BILL)

(He nodded' his head no)

No we having seen anything violet yet, if that's what you mean, answer he respectful, while he were still watching the tape.

(DIALOGUE)

Then instantly they all saw BRUCE enter the store, and they celearly saw him murder GARCIA on camer. REYNOLDS jumped up in shock, SCOTT looked straight at BILL.

(SCOTT)

BILL, make copy's of this guy's face at once, we really do need to get him off the street as fast as we all can. said he responsible. (Looking at REYNOLDS and STEIN, with his right hand in his pocket.)

(DIALOGUE)

Just as SCOTT, REYNOLDS, and STEIN started to walk out REYNOLDS pause, looking at that guy's face on the TV monitor and looking down at the floor.

(REYNOLDS)

wait a minute lieutenant, with her left hand on his right arm looking at him. lieutenant, that guy's face, I know I have seen it some where, I just don't remember where right now. said her with irritation.)

(SCOTT)

MICHELLE, if you do remember let me know at once ok. (said and asked he with respect.)

(They are now walking out)

(STEIN)

Lieutenant, you will be the first to know, we promise you that, right MICHELLE. (said he with sincere credibly.)

(DIALOGUE)

As they all climbed the stairs back to the first floor, lieutenant MACK went on out about his business. REYNOLDS and STEIN stopped at the front door.

(REYNOLDS)

By the way STEIN what did the two girl's have to say? Asked her seriously?)

(STEIN)

From what I gather from them, they absolute did not see any of that transmission of that killing, the two of them just simply walk in the store to buy candy, and some soft drink's, when they found that guy dead, ((Answer him with concern)

(They walked on out)

(DIALOGUE)

SLUG-LINE

INT-NEXT-MORNING AT HEADQUARTER'S

Doing a briefing, MICHELLE and STEIN found copy's of the suspect picture's in the lieutenant squad room office's, where BILL left them. MICHELLE talk's to uniform police officer's. (STEIN passing out suspect picture.)

(REYNOLDS STANDING ARM'S FOLD)

Office's the picture you have in your hand, we really do need you to watch out for this guy. Especially you that work's this area or close to that area, or in the region of that area, he is charge with first degree murder and first degree robbery, we need to get him as fast as we can ok. if you see this guy do not hesitate to make the arrest on him, then call me (she look's at STEIN) or

STEIN here. thank you all very much, see you later. (They all nodded yes and walked on out with the picture.)

SLUG-LINE-NEW SCENE (DIALOGUE)
THREE DAYS LATER
EXT-DAY-TIME—With other traffic and people on the street's. While STEIN and MICHELLE were patrolling the street's in chapel Hill.

(STEIN)
Hey MICHELLE, look at that guy there at the gas station, (said he, A little excited, as he were driving slow.)
(she look's at the photo, then at the guy.)

(REYNOLDS)
STEIN, that's him. (answer her excited, letting the squad passenger car window down.)

(DIALOGUE)
They quickly pull's in there and exit out the car, walking to BRUCE and showing their badge's. (BRUCE look's at them.)

(REYNOLDS)
Sir is this you?(asked her? showing him a photo of him.)

(BRUCE)
Yes that's me why?(he look's at her, putting his hand on his hip.) just what the hell you people want with me? (answer and asked he with a nasty attitude.)

(STEIN)
Sir, do you have any ID on you?(asked he with a straight face) BRUCE look's at him, reaching in his hip pocket showing his driver license.)

(CONT)
(STEIN)

Mr. HAGAN, if you would just come on down town with us, we will tell you all about it. (said he)

(BRUCE)

Down town, for what? why you people can not find a fucking thing else to do, accept slender a good citizen like me. I having done not a fucking thing wrong man. and what about my fucking car? (said and asked he loud.)

(CONT REYNOLDS)

Mr. HAGAN, shut your mouth, we will take care of your car, STEVE, put him in the back seat now, right now. (said her in a strong voice, pointing her finger at them.)

(DIALOGUE)

(STEIN put's his right hand on BRUCE shoulder, as he begins to walk BRUCE to their car.)

(STEIN)

Mr. HAGAN, we just need you to come on down town with us, so we can talk to you about a murder and robbery. But right now I need you to put your hands behind you. I'M putting these handcuffs on you for your safety and mine. (said he with serious frustration.)

(BRUCE)

Murder, robbery, you people must be crazy then hell itself, with your fucking stupid ass charges against me. (said he angry and loud, as other people were pumping gas were looking at him.)

(DIALOGUE)

(After being handcuff by STEIN, BRUCE got in the back seat of their car, quietly angry.)

(CONT DIALOGUE)

After MICHELLE, removed BRUCE car away from the gas pump's to the side of the building. A medium tall Caucasian women name LUCY exit out of the station, MICHELLE were walking back to her car.)

(LUCY)

Hey you there?(asked her in a normal voice.))

(CONT MICHELLE)
(CONT)
(REYNOLDS stop's looking at LUCY.)

(REYNOLDS)

Are you talking to me?(asked her in a normal voice?)

(CONT LUCY)

Yes I'm, if that car set there longer than one hour, it will be setting on the back of a flat bed towing truck. This not a junk yard you know. (answer and said her with frustration, pointing her finger at REYNOLDS.)

(CONT REYNOLDS)

Fine, make all charge's to that guy in the back seat
(answer her getting into her car.)

(DIALOGUE)

(They leave the scene, for headquarters with BRUCE.)

SLUG-LINE-INT
HEAD-QUARTERS-SAME-DAY
INTERROGATION-ROOM-ONE
NEW-SCENE-OTHER POLICE OFFICER AND PEOPLE IN HALLWAY AND OFFICER

(REYNOLDS)

Mr. HAGAN, where were you three night ago around 9'PM? (asked her serious? setting across the table from BRUCE)

(BRUCE)

I don't know, I might have been at home watching T.V. or taking a shower or something. (answer he leaning back in his chair, his arms fold frustrate angry.)

(STEIN)

Well, we have a witness putting you at a store involve with a shooting. (said he, walking around the table, having a seat on the corner, looking at BRUCE.)

(DIALOGUE)

In walk's the assistant D.A, Caucasian medium tall man name Mr. JAMES FUTCH. STEIN introduces him to Mr. BRUCE HAGAN.

(FUTCH) STANDING

Mr. HAGAN, do you understand what you are being charge with? (asked he with a straight face.)

(BRUCE)

Just what in the hell, you people are trying to charge me with? (answer he with irritation?)

(FUTCH)

Sir, we have you on tape, robbing a store and killing the clerk. (said he looking direct at BRUCE.)

(instantly BRUCE jump's up.)

Man, I never did such a thing like that, and if you saying I did, I want a lawyer right now. (answer he in a loud angry voice.)

(CONT FUTCH)

with the acceptance of attorney or not, you charge this man with first degree murder and robbery right now. (said he, with the expression of irritation.)

(CONT)

(The D.A. turned and walked out.)

(REYNOLDS) STANDING

Please stand up Mr. HAGAN?(asked her?)

(STEIN put's the handcuff on BRUCE.)

(CONT REYNOLDS)

Mr. HAGAN, you are under arrest for first degree murder, and first degree robbery. Sir you have the right to remain silent, you also have the right to have a attorney present doing question, if you can not afford one, then one will be a pointed to you by the court's, sir do you understand these right. (said and asked her in a strong voice.)

(BRUCE nodded his head yes.)

(STEIN and REYNOLDS walked BRUCE to the jail cell, and locked him up for the night.)

NEW-SCENE
SLUG-LINE-NEXT-MORNING (DIALOGUE)
INT-ARRANGEMENT-COURT
REPRESENTING-Mr. BRUCE HAGAN-NANCY ELLIOTT-ATTORNEY-CAUCASIAN MEDIUM-TALL
PRESIDING-JUDGE-SAM MASON-CAUCASIAN-TALL
TRANSCRIPT-RECORDER-MARTHA JONES-CAUCASIAN-MEDIUM-TALL
COURT-ROOM-REPORTER-MONICA BALL-AFRICAN-AMERICAN-MEDIUM-TALL
SHERIFF-GEORGE BLUE-ON-DUTY-CAUCASIAN-MEDIUM-TALL
OTHER PEOPLE IN COURT ROOM. SEATED DOWN

(MONICA) STANDING

Your honor, docket number 02310 the state of north Carolina, verse one Mr. BRUCE HAGAN, the charge is murder in the first degree of one GARCIA LOPEZ, robbery in the first degree of one seven eleven store. (said her in a normal voice.)

(CONT MONICA)
(she give's paper work to judge SAM MASON.)
(JUDGE MASON)SEATED DOWN

Murder, robbery, all in the first degree?
Miss ELLIOTT, nice to see you again. (said he in a strong voice.)

(NANCY) STANDING
Same here judge. (answer her in a normal voice.)

(CONT JUDGE)
Miss ELLIOTT, I need a plead?(asked he?)

(NANCY)
Not guilty your honor. (answer her.)
(The judge look's at the D.A.)

(CONT JUDGE)
Bail Mr. FUTCH) (asked he?)

(FUTCH) STANDING
Your honor the state is requesting remained or a one million dollars bail, because of this man criticism and reputation against other people, killing innocent people as well as robbing them. He has no respect and has not showed any remorse for the crime he has committed. He's a serious threat to our community. (said he seriously in a normal voice.)

(instantly NANCY responded)
Your honor one million dollars would be a revoked hardship on my client. He has lived here all his life, and he has family here, he also work's here and he pay's tax's here as well. (said her seriously, looking at the D.A.)

(CONT JUDGE)
And no one provoked him to go out, murder and rob innocent people either. (asked and said he, with a angry voice and face, looking straight at NANCY and BRUCE.) STANDING

(CONT JUDGE)
(judge look's at BRUCE with a straight face.)
Mr. HAGAN, you are here by order not to leave orange county or the state of north Carolina until trial. Do you under stand me sir?(said and asked he, in a normal voice?)

(BRUCE)
Yes sir your honor, I do. (answer he responsible, looking at the judge.)

(CONT JUDGE)
Good, real good, bail is set at ten thousand dollars, cash or bond, next case. (said he, as he tap his gavel turned paper work down on his desk, leaning back in his chair.)

(instantly CONT FUTCH)

Your honor this man is charge with first degree murder, and robbery, there is no insurance he will not go out, kill and rob again. How can you set bail so low?(asked he in a loud frustration voice, with both of his hand's out in front of him.)

(CONT JUDGE)

(He set up straight, clear his throat)

Mr. FUTCH, you better lower your voice, you are real close of being held in contempt of court. This is my court room and I will do what I want to in here. Do you understand me sir?(said and asked he in a normal voice, looking at him?)

(CONT FUTCH)

Yes your honor I do, I'm sorry judge, but judge I was only looking out for the public and the people of orange county safety. (answer he with frustration, looking at the judge.)

(CONT JUDGE)

Good, next case. (answer he clearly.)

(DIALOGUE)

As sheriff BLUE, were leading BRUCE out of the court room. NANCY and FUTCH walked out into the hallway, over to one side standing.

(FUTCH looking at her.)

NANCY, I'm going to put your client away for a very long time. I'm also thinking about filing a motion for capital punishment as well. (said he seriously)

(NANCY)

JAMES, the trial have not even started yet, and you already claiming a conviction. (she smile) JAMES, even the high bail you ask for went wrong for you. (said her laughing as she walk's away, down the hall.)

NEW-SCENE (DIALOGUE)
SLUG-LINE
INT-EXT-THREE-NIGHT-LATER-CHAPEL-HILL-N.C.
BRUCE HAGAN-APARTMENT-ELMWOOD-CIR.

A black Mercedes car arrived outside at 12'30AM, secret justice in car, put's on black ski mass and black glove's, screw silence on barrel of 9mm gun, exit out of car, quietly, walk's up to apartment window look's in window see BRUCE coming out of bathroom on first floor, down the hall toward the bedroom window, secret justice pump's two shot's through window into BRUCE chest, killing him instantly, secret justice take's out black handkerchief, wipe's barrel of gun off, enter car, leave scene quietly.

NEW-SCENE (DIALOGUE)
SLUG-LINE-NEXT-MORNING-8'AM
INT-EXT-BRUCE-APARTMENT

BRUCE girlfriend arrived at his apartment, name SUSAN MERRITT. (Caucasian medium tall.) using her key, she open the door and finds BRUCE in the hallway dead, she dial 911 immediately forensic other police officer's, REYNOLDS and STEIN arrived on the scene. STEIN stopped outside talking to other officer's. REYNOLDS enter the apartment.

While uniform police officer's were putting up yellow crime tape outside the apartment, and some other officer's had started a canvas around the neighbor hood. As 'she enter the apartment she saw forensic AIL were taking picture of BRUCE and the crime scene. She also could see the decease laying flat on his back between the bedroom door, and the hallway. She walk's up to forensic AIL.

(REYNOLDS)

AIL, what do we know about this killing right now? (asked her sincere, standing looking at AIL, also standing)

(AIL)

MICHELLE, it look's like this guy took two in the chest through that window. (He pointed at bedroom window.)

(CONT AIL)

right there, sometime between midnight and. 1'AM this morning, from what I can tell. (answer he intelligent)

REYNOLDS)

AIL, do we know who this guy is?
(asked her sincere, a little loud?)

(AIL)

(He take's a step toward her as he lower his voice, looking at her.) MICHELLE, I think the women in the kitchen with ROY, I don't know who she is. maybe his wife or girlfriend. I don't know that either right now. I'm sure she can answer all of you question about what happen here also give you this guy's name as well. (answer he with a straight face.)

(REYNOLDS)

So there were no sign of force entrance?
(asked her, nodded her head no?)

AIL)

I don't think so MICHELLE.
(answer he a little frustrate loud, nodding his head no, as he turn away continue taking picture with his camera.)

(DIALOGUE)

REYNOLDS turned around and walked toward the kitchen door. She looked in. SUSAN setting at the kitchen table, officer ROY, standing by the kitchen door, SUSAN looking down at the floor, very histrionics and sad. REYNOLDS take's two step's in.

(CONT REYNOLDS)

REYNOLDS showed her badge, looking at SUSAN. Excuse—me miss, (SUSAN look's up)

I'm homicide detective MICHELLE REYNOLDS, I would like to ask you a few question about what happen here.

(SUSAN nodded yes)

How do you know the decease, do you guy's live together, are you married, just what?(asked her seriously, in a. soft normal voice, looking at her?)

(SUSAN)

My name is SUSAN MERRITT (nodding no) no we are not married, we did not live together either. the decease name is BRUCE HAGAN, I'm his girlfriend, I live over on kay street. all I know is when I let myself in this morning, I found BRUCE, laying in the hallway floor dead. (soft tear's) I just don't understand why would anyone wanted to hurt him. (nodded her head no.) I just dial 911. he were such a nice guy. (answer her very sensitive, looking at her.)

(REYNOLDS)

(She fold her arm's walking toward her slow.) Do you know if he recently had any enemy's, or were he having any trouble at work with his employer, or with another employee, did he do any drug's or drink alcohol, did he give you any reason, he maybe involve with someone else, other than yourself?(asked her with direct sincere, looking into her eye's?)

(SUSAN)

(she stand's up, wipe her eye's with her hand's, she fold her arm's.)

(CONT SUSAN VERY SERIOUS)

Hey look detective, I don't know what kind of consequences you are getting at. (left hand on her waste point's finger on other hand.) I never knew BRUCE to cheat on me. He were always straight with me and I with him. I found him to be a very intelligent loving man. I never expected him to be a victim of a brutality murder. (she nodded her head)thank you said her with frustration. BRUCE never had any enemy's that I knew of. He were well liked by everyone. (said her with a straight face.)

(REYNOLDS)

Alright I understand, (nodded yes) But what were your reason for coming here this morning? (asked her a little loud?)

(SUSAN)

On every Friday morning I always come by to pick up his dirty laundry. But by the time I get here, he would be already at work in Hillsborough. (answer her a little irritate)

(REYNOLDS)

When were the last time you saw him or talk to him? (asked her?)

(SUSAN)

He give me a call around 10'PM last night. He did not sound like something were wrong. (answer her, she look's at ROY.)

(REYNOLDS)

Did he seem like he were depress or stress about anything at all? (asked her with a straight face?)

(CONT SUSAN)

I have never knew him to be having any unfortunately dilemma of such behavior of that kind. (said her a little loud.)

(DIALOGUE)

(Suddenly STEIN enter the apartment into the kitchen where he heard voice's, SUSAN walk's over to kitchen sink, leaning her butt against it looking at them.)

(SUSAN)

Who is this guy?(asked her, looking at REYNOLDS, running her left finger's through her hair, looking at STEIN?)

(REYNOLDS)

This is homicide detective STEIN. (answer her with one of her hand in her pant's pocket.)

(STEIN)

As he take's two step's toward SUSAN showing his badge, he look's at officer ROY.) officer ROY,(he look's at STEIN.) I think officer PETE need you outside. (said he in a normaly voice.) (ROY nodded yes, leave's)

(REYNOLDS)

About how long you've been seeing each other?
(asked her?)

(SUSAN)

For the pass two year's. (answer her.)

(CONT SUSAN)

Detective, why are you talking to me like this? Are you trying to make me a suspect, while the man I love he is laying on his floor dead. (said her a little excited. she take's one step toward her, pointed her first finger at her.) The detective let me tell you something. I loved BRUCE and he loved me, I had no reason to hurt him or kill him, while you are standing here wasting my time and yours, you need to be out there finding the responsible person and why I'm sure his family they will want to know and so do I. (said her a little excited irritate.)

(REYNOLDS)
(she look's at STEIN)

SUSAN here, she found the body this morning, you want believe who it is. go take a look. (said her serious.)

(DIALOGUE)

STEVE walk's down the hall to see the body, and then back to them with a surprise face.)

(STEIN)

MICHELLE, is that's the guy we arrested the other day on a murder charge?(asked he?)

(SUSAN had a very surprise look on her face, looking at them.)

(REYNOLDS)

He's the one it seems our boy here, he had a enemy, his girl or we did not know about, he took two in the chest some time last night through that window at end of the hall.

(said her with a caution attitude.)

(STEIN)

MICHELLE, let's go see what we can find out. I'm sure AIL and the rest of them can finish up here. (said he serious.)

(CONT DIALOGUE)

(They leave the apartment and after enter the car.)

(STEIN)

MICHELLE, I'm sorry that guy lost his life, and to say this But what go's around, come around as well. (said he with a straight face.)

(REYNOLDS)

You know STEIN, I can appreciate what you just said, because when my grandmother were around, she would always tell us, you will reap what you sow (said her with absolute compassion.)

(DIALOGUE)

(As forensic and other police officer's were canvassing, STEIN started the car up and they leave the scene.)

NEW SCENE (DIALOGUE)
SLUG-LINE
TWO-DAYS-LATER
FORENSIC-AUTOPSY-EXAMI NATION-ROOM

Two day's later REYNOLDS and STEIN talked to the forensic autopsy examinate EMILY FULTON ((Caucasian medium tall) in the examination room.) As they enter the room, EMILY talking on the phone. BRUCE HAGAN body in the freezer.

(EMILY)

Ok, I will get back with you, right now I have people here I need to talk to, by-by. (said her)

(she hang's up and walk's over to them.)

(STEIN)

EMILY what can you tell us about Mr. BRUCE HAGAN death?(asked he serious)

(DIALOGUE)

She walks over and pick's up a file from her desk. She take's a deep breath, and walk's over to them.)

(EMILY)

What I found out about Mr. BRUCE HAGAN, he had enough cocaine in his system that would make any one do crazy thing's. I doubt if this guy knew what day of the week it was, or what he were doing at all time's. (said her with a sense of concern.)

(REYNOLDS)

EMILY, let me see that file. (EMILY hand's it to her.) REYNOLDS look's at it.) STEIN, I think this man had his girlfriend fool about his drug used, and he just may have had an enemy some where as well. (said her serious, looking at him.)

(STEIN)
(nodding yes)

I think you are right MICHELLE, because there is a reason when someone is kill. But the question is why did someone kill him?(asked he looking at her and EMILY, and they looking stun at him.)

NEW-SCENE (DIALOGUE)
SLUG-LINE-ONE WEEK LATER
COURT ROOM-ARRANGEMENT
ATTORNEY-LISA LANIER(CAUCASIAN MEDIUM TALL
CLIENT-GINA ADAMS(CAUCASIAN MEDIUM TALL
OTHER PEOPLE IN COURT ROOM.

(MONICA)

Your honor case number 11229, the state verse one GINA ADAMS. The charge is listening for the propose of prostitution, a hazard to the public. (said her reading the charge, in a normal voice.)

(she give's paper work to judge SAM MASON.)

(JUDGE)

Mrs. LANIER, so your client is a hazard to the public? how do she plead? (asked he generalist, looking at her?)

(LANIER)

Not guilty your honor, (answer her respectfully.)

(CONT JUDGE)

Miss ADAMS, how do you feel, of what you do? (asked he with a irritation face and voice?)

(GINA)
(left hand on her hip)

Your honor, a girl got eat and pay rent.

(answer her with no shame, court room laughing.)

(CONT JUDGE)

And there is no other line of work, you can get into, such as Walmart or a grocery store clerk?

(asked he?)

(CONT GINA)

Your honor I've been looking for work, for over a year, but nothing have turned up. (Nodded no answer her responsible.)

(CONT JUDGE)

(He look's at the D.A.)

Bail Mr. FUTCH?

(asked he?)

(FUTCH)

Your honor, the state is asking for the a mount of bail of five thousand dollars, because of this women hazard profession to the public, (answer he serious.)

(CONT JUDGE)

Miss ADAMS, you are here by order not to leave orange county or the state of north Carolina, do you under stand me mam?(said and asked he with a straight face)

(CONT GINA)

Yes your honor, I do. (answer her responsible.)

(CONT JUDGE)

Good, bail is set at five hundred dollars, cash or bond next case. (said he, tap his gavel with a straight face)

(DIALOGUE)

(instantly waving one hand in the air)

(CONT FUTCH)

JUDGE, what is your problem judge, that bail is to low, this women(pointed his finger at GINA)) COULD BE SPREADING dangerous deception defect S.T.D by having sex with the public, even giving someone the H.I.V, virus. (said he in a very loud angry voice.)

(CONT JUDGE)

(jumping up from his chair)

Mr. FUTCH, I told you before, this is my court room. if you do not like how I do business or how I run it, then you need to stay the hell out of here. (He looked at attorney LANIER) Mrs. LANIER take your client and get the hell out of here. (said he in a very loud angry voice)

(DIALOGUE)

(As they all were leaving the court room, the D.A. looked at the JUDGE)

NEW-SCENE (DIALOGUE)
SLUG-LINE-ONE-WEEK-LATER
EXT-INT-11'3OPM-E FRANKLIN ST-TUESDAY

A black Mercedes car pull's a long a side walk, secret justice in side car, see's a prostitute with a black short dress on, the passenger car window go's down, she bend down and look's in.

(GINA)

Hello there, I did not think I would never see you again. Do you need to see me in private? (GINA nodded her head yes) She open the car door and get's in, car pull's away from side walk.

(CONT GINA)

I have a room around the corner at the days inn. (said her excited ready to make easily money)

(DIALOGUE)

car pull's into hotel parking lot, in front of room 101 GINA exit out of car, unlock room door, she go's in, leaving room door open, secret justice put's on black glove's screw silence on barrel of 9mm gun, exit out of car, walk's to room door with gun in hand, watch GINA turning bed down she look's up.

(CONT GINA)

Put that thing away, come on, we are going to have a good time. (said her all smile's) secret justice take's one step into the room. As GINA started to unzip her dress, looking at secret justice, secret justice pump's two shot's into her chest, killing her instantly, as she fall's across the bed face down eye's open. secret justice take's out black handkerchief, wipe barrel of gun off. As secret justice exit out of room, closed door behind, leave scene quietly.

NEW-SCENE (DIALOGUE)
SLUG-LINE-NEXT-MORNING-AT-
DAYS-INN-ROOM-101
EXT-INT-SUNSHINE-11'AM
HOTEL-MANAGER-ED FRAZIER-CAUCASIAN-SHORT-REAL FAT MAN
CLEANING-LADY-RENEE-MEXICAN

(DIALOGUE)

A Mexican cleaning maid women short name RENEE, that Wednesday morning knocked on room 101 door to clean it, but there were no answer. As she used her master key to enter in, again she knocked and call out house keeper, and again there were no answer. As she pushed the door open, she could see GINA ADAMS laying across the bed with lot's of blood on the sheet's, with loud scream's she ran to manager office's, as she reached the office, just about nervously out of breath, she busted through the door, as ED sitting at his desk having some coffee.

(RENEE)
Mr, Mr. ED, I think someone die in room 101.
(said her very scare excited frustrate)
(ED jumped up from his chair)

(ED)
calm down my child, holding her by her shoulder's)
(said he with passion, looking at her.)

(CONT ED)
(RENEE almost breathlee)
RENEE, what did you just say?
(asked he serious?)

(CONT RENEE)
(A little calm)
Mr. ED, I think someone die in room 101.
(said her serious)

(CONT ED)
excited, someone die, you stay here, I'll go see.
(said he)

(DIALOGUE)
(ED, walked down to room 101 and saw GINA, he returned to his office and call the police with RENEE.)

(DIALOGUE)
With in minutes police, forensic, along with REYNOLDS and STEIN arrived on the scene. As they exited out of their car, uniform police officer were putting up yellow crime tape around the crime scene front door. REYNOLDS call out to officer ROY and PETE. (they looked at her.

(REYNOLDS)
Let's get a canvas started right way ok.

(said her with caution)

(STEIN)

MICHELLE, while I check out the crime scene room, why don't you go to the manager office and see if anyone know anything or saw something about this crime. (said he serious looking at her.)

(REYNOLDS)

(nodded her head yes)

Yeah STEVE, I will(As she walking away from him, and he begin walking to room door. STEVE, I really do hope we finds some fast answer this time. (said her serious, she wave at him.)

(DIALOGUE)

As he enter the crime room, REYNOLDS reached the manager office and enter in also. ED standing as RENEE sitting in a chair drinking, a cup water, still looking stun.

(REYNOLDS)

(she showed her badge)

Hi my name is MICHELLE REYNOLDS, I'm the homicide detective working this case. can one of you tell me what happen here last night.

(ED)

This is one of my cleaning lady here(pointed one hand toward RENEE.)her name is RENEE, and when she went into clean that room, a little while a go, she found that women dead.

(said he honestly)

(As MICHELLE started to take note's)

Sir, what is your name?

(CONT REYNOLDS)

(asked her serious?)

(CONT ED)

My name is ED FRAZIER, I'm the manager here. (answer he.)

(CONT REYNOLDS)

Sir, did you or do you know anyone who may know this women?(asked her?)

(CONT ED)

(As he crossed his chest with his right hand) Mother of GOD, I did not know her personal. I only saw her regular especial at night.

(answer he.)

(CONT REYNOLDS))

Sir, would anyone else would be with her, when you saw her at night?

(asked her?)

(CONT ED)

At all time's of night, she would have all different, kind of men's with her.

(Nodded yes, answer he gently)

(CONT REYNOLDS)

Did you notice if she had someone with her last night sir?

(asked her?)

(CONT ED)

I'm sorry, but I did not see her at all last night.

(answer he)

(CONT REYNOLDS)

(she looked at RENEE)

Sir, can your cleaning lady speak English?

(asked her?)

(RENEE nodded yes, pushing her hair back with her left hand.)

(CONT REYNOLDS)

RENEE, were anyone else in the room or bath room when you arrived there?

(asked her?)

(RENEE)

(nodded no)

No mam, I saw no one in room, but that lady on bed shot. (answer her serious.)

(CONT REYNOLDS)

Did you happen to notice anyone setting in a car outside or leaving in a car? (asked her?)

(CONT RENEE)

(nodded no)

I saw no one at all, I just ran here to office, to tell Mr. ED here what I saw in room 101, that's all.
(answer her.)

(REYNOLDS take's out one of her card's and hand's it to ED.)

(CONT REYNOLDS)

Sir if you or RENEE, think of anything at all, please do not hesitate to give me a call at once, and thank you-all for talking to me. (said her with a small smile.) (she turn around and walked out.)

(DIALOGUE)

As MICHELLE, reached the crime room were STEIN and forensic AIL were taking picture's and gathering other evidence, she enter the room. As officer ROY and PETE with other officer were constantly knocking on other hotel door's and canvas a two block area around the hotel, STEIN walk over to the in side door where she were standing. AIL were putting GINA small shoulder black pocket book in a big brown paper bag.

(REYNOLDS)
AIL,(He look's at her) Do we have a time of death yet?
(asked her?)

(AIL)
It look's to me sometime around midnight last night. I also can tell you this(He walked over to the bed, pointing his finger at the body) this women here she die a very violet death at close range. (nodded yes) MICHELLE, I'm thinking she must knew her assassin, because I found no sign of sexual assault as you can see her clothes has not been remove, her panties were never touch. back at the house EMILY may find out more about her on the table, my question is, what did she do for this to happen to her?
(said and asked he, looking at her and she at him.)

(STEIN)
(standing beside her)

(CONT STEIN)
MICHELLE, get this, there is a little over nine hundred dollars in her little black pocket book.
(said he serious)

(REYNOLDS)
(excited, looking at him.)
Nine hundred dollars? STEVE, do you think she were a working girl?
(asked her?)

(STEIN)
MICHELLE, when we get to the station I will personal run a back ground check on her.
(said he)

(REYNOLDS)
By the way, how ROY and PETE doing with the canvassing

(asked her?)

(STEIN)

Since AIL and I have been here, they have not found not one witness to this crime.

(answer he)

(CONT STEIN)

MICHELLE, this is the second body, we have with in a week and there were no force entrance (He pointed at inside door)

(REYNOLDS)

I can see that myself, (looking at AIL)
(said her) (nodded yes)

(CONT STEIN)

I'm beginning to feel a little shame, with all this canvassing going on, knocking on door's and no one seen or heard nothing at all, especial when we heaven found any witness behind all of this killing yet. (said he, a little angry.)

(CONT REYNOLDS)

Oh yeah, you know STEIN, we may have a serial killer on our hands or someone, who have their own jurisdiction secret justice going on. But what I want to know is this, what are their person or person quote, unquote, motive for all of this killing. (said her with a compassionate straight face and voice.)

(DIALOGUE)

(REYNOLDS and STEIN leave's the scene, leaving forensic AIL and other police to finish up.)

(DIALOGUE)

After MICHELLE and STEIN arrived back at the police station, STEIN kept his promise and ran a back ground check on GINA. It turned out miss GINA ADAMS had been arrested four time's that year for prostitution.

NEW-SCENE—(DIALOGUE)
SLUG-LINE-ONE-MONTH-LATER-HILLSBOROUGH-NC.
INT-EXT-918'AM-THURSDAY-MORNING
CHARACTER-BRYANT WINSLOW-AFRICAN-AMERICAN-MEDIUM-TALL
CHARACTER-DALLAS JAMES-AFRICAN-AMERICAN-MEDIUM-TALL
CHARACTER-ERNEST WESLEY-AFRICAN-AMERICAN-MEDIUM-TALL
CHARACTER-MARY WILSON-CAUCASIAN-MEDIUM-TALL-BANK-TELLER
OTHER CUSTOMERS IN THE BANK AT THIS TIME.

The first guy through the bank door's were DALLAS, where he throw a black gum bag on the counter in front of bank teller MARY WILSON. Hurry up women, put the fucking money in the damn bag, hurry up bitch, hurry up, the rest of you get down on the damn floor right now. (meaning the other teller's and customer's) while BRYANT and ERNEST holding their gun's on them. bitch you better clean all those draws out, only the paper money. If you put one of those little red bags in there I'm coming back to see you personal. MARY been' so nervous going as fast as she can to meet his demands, she gave him the bag containing about ten thousand dollars. They ran out and just as they were leaving one of the unknown customer wrote down the jeep license tag number. After MARY dial 911, police and the A.T.F. squad team arrived very fast on the scene, where the unknown customer gave the tag number to the police. The three robber's made it back to ERNEST WESLEY parents house on Farrington RD, just off HWY 86 south, out back in the storage room, where they count the money up, ten thousand dollars.

(After they spitted the money up)

(BRYANT)

Alright my brothers(excited) it is time to live a little. (said he all smile's)

(ERNEST)

BRYANT, you never been so right, (answer he exited smiling)

(DALLAS)

Hey, look here my brothers, I told you I will-pull it off,(They are giving each other high five and touching their fists together.) But right now I need me 40, colt 45 and a Newport cigarette, now where is the damn store. (said he real exited)

(BRYANT)

That way,(pointed his two left fingers) come on let's ride. (said he.)

(DALLAS)

No, we walk, let that jeep sit there for right now. we will get rid of it later, after dark.

(said he serious)

(They had stole the blue Cherokee 1997 jeep from a near by shopping mall.)

(DIALOGUE)

They all walked to the corner store. Late that night around 11'30 PM all three of them riding together. they were riding around trying to find a place to dish the jeep. But when DALLAS turned on to southwood DR, police turn on his blue lights and stopped them. (one police car behind and one police car in front of them. They all were instantly arrested for first degree bank robbery, and they had lot's of cash money with them.

(DIALOGUE)

NEW-SCENE
SLUG-LINE-NEXT-MORNING-FRIDAY
INT-COURT-ROOM-ARRANGEMENT
ATTORNEY-DONALD OLIVE-AFRICAN-AMERICAN-TALL
COURT ROOM FULL OF OTHER PEOPLE AND ATTORNEYS, SOME PEOPLE WERE STANDING AROUND THE WALL"S.

(MONICA)

Your honor, docket number 119208, the state verse one BRYANT WINSLOW, robbery in the first degree, one DALLAS JAMES, robbery in the first degree, and one ERNEST WESLEY, robbery in the first degree. All three defendant are charge with robbing one city bank of Hillsborough All three defendant are represented by one attorney Mr. DONALD OLIVE.

(DIALOGUE)
(She give's paper work to judge SAM MASON)

(JUDGE)

Mr. OLIVE,(nodded his head) I having seen you in a while. (said he in a strong voice, looking at him.)

(Mr. OLIVE, standing with his client's)

That's true your honor, I've been real busy here lately judge.
(answer he honestly)

(CONT JUDGE)

Mr. OLIVE, how do all three of your client's plead?
(asked he?)

(Mr. OLIVE)

Not guilty, on all count's your honor, (respectfully answer he) (judge look's at the D.A.)

(CONT JUDGE)

Application for bail Mr. FUTCH?

(asked he in a strong voice, looking at him?)

(FUTCH STANDING)

Your honor, due to the nature of this crime, these three defendant willing robbed city bank of Hillsborough, pointing gun's, into innocent people face's terrorization them. Your honor, the state is requesting remained or a one million dollars each on bail. (answer he in a calm voice)

(CONT OLIVE)

(instantly looking at the judge) Your honor, one million dollars is extremely out of the question.

(His right hand out in front of him) your honor, these guy's have never been in trouble before. All three of them have and comes from good family's back ground, your honor I don't think they would be of any flight risk. your honor, one million dollars is very much presidential against these three gentleman. (said he with a serious explanation of concern)

(CONT JUDGE)

Very much presidential he said. (JUDGE looked down at paper work and started to write)

(CONT JUDGE)

Mr. WINSLOW, Mr. JAMES, and Mr. WESLEY you are here by order not to leave orange county or the state of North Carolina until trial Do I make myself clear to you all?(said he with a straight face and voice.)

(ALL THREE DEFENDANT)

Yes your honor, you do. (respectfully, answer all three.)

(CONT JUDGE)

Good, bail is set at ten thousand dollars each, cash or bond next case. (said he, tap his gavel in a strong voice.)

(CONT FUTCH)

(instantly, taking a step toward the bench) JUDGE, have you totally lost your mind, you know that bail is at extremely to low. After they make bail they will be out robbing someone else or terrorization other people, what is wrong with you judge? (said he in a loud angry voice and ugly face.)

(CONT JUDGE)

Mr. FUTCH, I'm tide of you coming in my court room disrespecting my court room and me. get the hell out of here before I throw your ass in jail man. (shouted he in a loud angry voice.)

(DIALOGUE)

(FUTCH, turn to leave, he stop's and turned back around)

(CONT FUTCH)

JUDGE, I think it's about time, I contact the jurisdiction congressional committee and let them know, how hypocrite you have been to the people in orange county. letting criminal go on such low bail. (said he with a serious absolute frustration attitude.)

(CONT JUDGE)

Get out, get out, I said get out, The hell with the congressional committee, (shouted he with rage.)

(DIALOGUE)

BRYANT, DALLAS, and ERNEST all three posted bail that morning and were release.)

NEW-SCENE (DIALOGUE)
SLUG-LINE-ONE-MONTH-LATER
MONDAY-NIGHT-11'15PM
EXT
CHARCTER-WAYNE BROWN-AFRICAN-AMERICAN-TALL

As BRYANT, DALLAS, and ERNEST exit out of a pool room, A black Mercedes car, park's down the street. The three guy's seprate. BRYANT, and DALLAS walked south as ERNEST walked north on heathston LN. When secret justice notice this, put on ski mass and black glove's on hands, screw silence on barrel of 9mm gun, start car up, light's off, let car roll down the. streets slowly behind ERNEST quietly, let's passenger car window down, stop's beside ERNEST. ERNEST bended down and look's into car. secret justice pump's two shot's into his chest, killing him instantly. secret justice Pick's up black handkerchief, wipe's barrel of gun off, leave's scene quietly with light's on.

REMAIN-SAME-SCENE (DIALOGUE)
EXT-NIGHT

As the pool room owner WAYNE were leaving, for the night walking to his car, parked on the street, he found ERNEST WESLEY on the sidewalk dead, and he call the police with his cell phone.

(DIALOGUE)

Forensic AIL, REYNOLDS, STEIN, with other uniform police officer's arrived on the scene with in minutes. As uniform police officer's immediately started putting up yellow crime tape, STEIN and REYNOLDS walked over to forensic AIL with the body.

(STEIN)

(He bended down and take's a wallet off the body, while MICHELLE looked on.)

(CONT STEIN)
(looking into the wallet)
MICHELLE, I have an I.D. here. could this be a robbery, there's no money here. (He looked at REYNOLDS) MICHELLE, his name is ERNEST WESLEY. He live on farrington RD. MICHELLE, I realize, to me it look's like the same M.O. as the last, (said he in a normal voice.)

(REYNOLDS)
(nodded yes)
It do look's that way, But I wonder if there were any witness this time. (said her, a little disturb.)
(She looked at AIL)

(CONT REYNOLDS)
AIL, about how long ago this man were kill?
(asked her?)
(AIL stood up)

(AIL)
MICHELLE, this guy were kill no more than ten minutes ago, with all this fresh blood spill on the ground here. (He walked around the body) you know MICHELLE, I'm thinking did this guy here had a bad criminal record, or were it was just an accident killing. A man in the wrong place at the wrong time, (said he with affection)

(REYNOLDS)
AIL, I'm sure after you get him on the table, EMILY will be able to tell us more about him.
(said her looking at him)

(DIALOGUE)
AIL, nodded yes as he bended back down continuing examine the body for evidence.
(STEIN looked at officer PETE)

(CONT STEIN)
Hey PETE, Do you know who call this in?
(asked he?)
(Officer PETE pointed to WAYNE)

(DIALOGUE)
(As REYNOLDS and STEIN walking over to WAYNE)

(REYNOLDS)
If this was not a robbery, I wonder what did he do to get shot? or was I right about a serial killer on our hands. (said her with affection)

(CONT REYNOLDS)
(They showed their badge's)
Sir, I'm detective REYNOLDS and this is my partner detective STEIN. Sir, what is your name?
(asked her?)

(WAYNE)
My name is WAYNE BROWN I'm the owner of that pool room right over there. (He pointed to it)
(said he.)

(CONT REYNOLDS)
Well Mr. BROWN, do you know this guy, were you all friends or what?(asked her serious?)

(WAYNE CONT)
No I did not know him personal, but he and two other guy's comes into my pool room regularly. In fact they came in together tonight.

(answer he in a normal voice.)
(REYNOLDS)
(exited)
Tow other guy's? did you see them leave's together tonight?

(CONT REYNOLDS)
What did these two other guy's look like?
(asked her?)

(CONT WAYNE)
Lady, I was not watching the clock on their arrival here and no I did not see them leave together tonight either. (answer he with a little attitude.)

(CONT WAYNE)
But normally they comes in together. The other two guy's are about his height and age, they are also two African American as well. (answer he, looking at her.)

(CONT REYNOLDS)
(looking at him with a straight face)
Have you ever notice any problem's or trouble between them?
(asked her?)

(CONT WAYNE)
Lady, I have never notice any problem's between them, they always seem to have a very good friendly relationship between them, from what I could see. They were always laughing and joking around with each other, about shooting pool.
(answer he.)

(STEIN)
So I'm taking it, you would not know where these two other guy's live as well? (asked he with a straight face?)

(CONT WAYNE)
Sorry, I sure don't. (answer he, shaking his head no.)

(CONT STEIN)
Thanks a lot for talking to us sir.
(said he.)

(DIALOGUE)
(REYNOLDS and STEIN walk's away toward their car)

(REYNOLDS)
STEVE, if what WAYNE just told us about this guy here is true then how did he end up like this dead? you know STEVE, I think it is time we get to the lab, and check with ballistics and see if the same weapon is responsible for all of this killing, first thing tomorrow morning ok. (asked and said her very content, looking at STEIN.)

(DIALOGUE)
(STEIN nodded yes, as they enter their car and leave the scene.)

SLUG-LINE-NEW-SCENE—(DIALOGUE)
INT-BALLISTICS-LAB
CHARACTER-TERSA BACON-CAUCASIAN-MEDIUM-TALL

(DIALOGUE)
(REYNOLDS and STEIN walked into the ballistics lab and had a conversation with the lab forensic Technology TERSA.)

(REYNOLDS)
(Looking at TERSA)
TERSA, what can you tell us about the gun or the bullet's EMILY pulled from Mr. WESLEY body?
(asked her serious?)

(DIALOGUE)
(TERSA walk's over and put's up a chart with light's on it against the wall.)

(TERSA)
(She is pointing with a pencil, looking at the chart)

If you look right here, these two bullet's came from the same gun. The first bullet enter the body, were the fatal shot. Look at the front of it, see how the front of it is push back a little, split on top a little. Now if you would come over here.

(REYNOLDS and STEIN look's through a microscope)

(REYNOLDS)

Yes I can see that.

(answer her.)

(CONT TERSA))

(She put's a second bullet under the scope)

Now look at the second bullet, it have a more of a soothing around head on it. (She looked at them) in other words that's because the second bullet follower direct behind the first bullet into the body, piercing the heart twice.

(said her serious)

(STEIN)

TERSA did you compare these two bullet's with any other bullet's you received in the pass from EMILY?

(asked he serious?)

(CONT TERSA)

STEVE, the other bullet's I had, I sent them to the F.B.I. lab sometime ago.

(answer her, looking at them.)

(DIALOGUE)

(REYNOLDS and STEIN had disappointed look's on their face's)

(REYNOLDS)

Alright TERSA, (She look's at STEIN) STEVE maybe we need to go talk to EMILY and see what she have to say about Mr. WESLEY Autopsy. (said her,) (They leave)

(DIALOGUE)

(STEIN and REYNOLDS enter the Autopsy examination room. EMILY coming out of a back room with both hands In her white coat pocket's walking toward them.)

(EMILY STANDING)

Hi MICHELLE, Hi STEVE. (said her smiling)

(STEVE and MICHELLE, STANDING)

Hi EMILY.

(answer them both smiling)

(EMILY)

Now, what can I do for you-all?

(asked her?)

(REYNOLDS)

EMILY, what have you find out about Mr. ERNEST WESLEY death?

(asked her seriously, looking at EMILY?)

(DIALOGUE)

(EMILY, walked to her desk and picked up a file and walked back to them. she open it.)

(EMILY)

I found out, Mr. WESLEY were shot at close range. He had lot's of gun powder on his clothes

(said her serious, looking at them.))

(STEIN)

EMILY, TERSA said both bullet's came from the same gun, is that right. (said and asked he seriously? looking at her)

(CONT EMILY)

That is right, you know something else, I did not find any illegal drugs in his blood or any illegal chemical in his body either. (nodded no) nothing at all. (answer her with professional affection.)

(CONT REYNOLDS)

(She folded her arms taking a step toward EMILY)

So he did not do drugs. You know something EMILY, I would like to know who in the hell is responsible for all this damn killing, and we can not find a witness at none of them. Thank a lot EMILY. Come on STEVE we better get back to the station. (said her with frustration of angry.)

NEW-SCENE—(DIALOGUE)
ERNEST-PARENTS-HOUSE
I NT-THREE-NIGHTS-LATER
CHARACTER-FATHER-JOHN WESLEY-AFRICAN-AMERICAN-MEDIUM-TALL
CHARACTER-MOTHER-HELEN WESLEY-AFRICAN-AMERICAN-SHORT
CHARACTER-SISTER-ANNIE WESLEY-AFRICAN-AMERICAN-SHORT
CHARACTER-BROTHER-HAROLD WESLEY-AFRICAN-AMERICAN-TALL

(DIALOGUE)

(The WESLEY family setting at the dining room table. JOHN, HELEN, ANNIE, and HAROLD.)

As DALLAS and BRYANT were paying their respect's as true friend's to ERNEST and his family, they had a conversation with Mr. WESLEY and his son HAROLD. other family member's, also other friend's are in the house too.)

(JOHN)

BRYANT, you knew ERNEST the long's of all of you boys. (HE looked straight at BRYANT.) son what could have impossible gone wrong for my son to end up dead like this?

(asked he with a very sad emotionally voice and face.)

(CONT BRYANT)

Mr. JOHN, all I can tell you is this, The last night we were leaving the pool room, ERNEST said he were going home, because you and him had talk about he need to find a job until our trial come around. (said he serious)

(JOHN nodded yes)

(HAROLD)

Coming home, were he alone or was somebody with him. If it were a drive by someone shot the wrong guy. (nodded no) (said he seriously, A little loud, looking at BRYANT and DALLAS.)

(DALLAS)

(standing just inside the dining room door)

HAROLD, Mr. JOHN, I don't understand this myself. (nodded no, he take's a step toward the table.)

I can not think of no time at all when ERNEST were having any trouble with anyone, or if he had a enemy. (nodded no) at no time at all. I'm sure you all knew how ERNEST liked joking around with everyone. (said he with a straight face and a serious voice.)

(ANNIE)

(She look at her DAD and MOM.)

DAD, I know for a fact ERNEST were not into drugs of any kind. He broke up with DENISE his girlfriend last year, after he found out she had cheated on him with someone else and got herself pregnant. (nodded no) I think ERNEST were in the wrong place at the wrong time, and someone just shot the wrong guy for no reason at all. (said her reaping a little, with her family looking at her)

(HELEN)
(She looked at her husband)
JOHN, I don't care who is responsible for this killing. My child is just as dead.
(said her very emotionally, with her family and friends looking at her.)

(CONT BRYANT)
Mr. JOHN, Mrs. HELEN, I'm sure you-all know ERNEST, DALLAS, and myself(He looked at DALLAS and back to them) has been our best friend since elementary school. I'm so sorry,(nodded no) this happen to ERNEST like this, and I have no answer why it did. (said he very sad emotionally)

(CONT DALLAS)
(He looked at the family)
Mr. JOHN, I know BRYANT and I are in trouble now with the law. But if I find out who did this to my best friend, I guarantee and I promise you, that person will answer to me instantly. (patted his self on the chest.) (said he.)

(CONT DALLAS)
Come on BRYANT, we better go, because I do not like this, (shaking his head no, with tear's running down his face, looking at BRYANT.)

(DIALOGUE)
(They leave.)

NEW-SCENE-(DIALOGUE)
SLUG-LINE-ONE-WEEK-LATER-NIGHT
EXT-SEVEN-ELEVEN-STORE-10'50
PM-MONDAY-FORESTHILL DR
CHARACTER-CHAD TAYLOR-CAUCASIAN-TALL_-CLERK

(CONT DIALOGUE)

As BRYANT came out of the store, in a hurry to get into his mother's dark blue 2003 Honda Accord car to leave, A black Mercedes car pulled in real fast, the passenger car window go's down, BRYANT bended down and look's into the car, secret justice with ski mass on pump's two shot's into his chest, killing him instantly, secret justice pick's up black handkerchief, wipe's barrel of gun off let's car window up leave's scene quietly.

(CONT DIALOGUE)

A few minutes later the store clerk name CHAD TAYLOR came out to throw his trash away and found BRYANT laying down beside the car, dead. instantly he went back inside the store and call the police. With in minutes forensic AIL and other forensic Technology, police, along with REYNOLDS and STEIN arrived on the scene. As AIL were checking the body for evidence, REYNOLDS and STEIN exited their car and walked slowly over to AIL.

(STEIN)

MICHELLE, I do not believe what is going on in our county. We have a very serious problem here, two people have been kill with in two week's apart, by who, why?

(asked and said he in a very serious normal voice.)

(REYNOLDS)

You know STEVE,(looking at him.) I don't understand it myself. What I really want to know, what is the motive for all this killing. But I do know something is going on, we do not know about. By the way have we started canvassing yet? if not, let's do that now, while I have a conversation with the store clerk, maybe we'll get lucky this time and find someone with some good information.

(DIALOGUE)

(As STEIN talked to ROY and PETE and other police officer's about starting a canvassing, REYNOLDS enter the store.)

(REYNOLDS)

(She showed her badge) (CHAD standing behind the counter, No other customer's in the store.)

Sir I'm detective REYNOLDS, what is your name sir? (asked her seriously?)

(CHAD)

My name is CHAD TAYLOR. (answer him in a nervous voice.)

(CONT REYNOLDS)

Mr. TAYLOR, will you please start from the beginning and tell me, just what did you see or hear tonight? (asked her very concern, looking at him.)

(CONT CHAD)

I did not see or hear anything at all, I just walked outside to throw the trash away and there that guy was, laying beside that car shot. (answer he seriously, looking at her.)

(CONT REYNOLDS)

Mr. TAYLOR, I know you are not that scared, even if you were no one is going to try and hurt you while, we are here. (The POLICE) (nodded no said her, looking at him.)

(CONT CHAD)

Lady, like I said, I walk through that door,(He pointed his finger) to throw the trash out, and I saw that guy laying there shot. (nodded no) No I did not see anyone or heard anything at all. (answer he a little irritate loud.)

(CONT REYNOLDS)

(she put's her left hand on her hip, she point's at CHAD, CHAD cough while smoking a cigarette, looking at her.)

Excuse me sir, I dare you to raise your voice to me again, I'm only here because a crime has been committee. And my job is to find out who is responsible for committee such crime. Do I make myself clear to you sir?(bobbing her head from side to side, (said her with the expression of frustration looking at him.)

(CONT CHAD)

Yes mam, I think I do. (nodded yes,, answer he with respect)

(CONT REYNOLDS)

(A little calm)

Now, did the decease have anyone else with him that you knew of sir?

(asked her looking at him.)

(CONT CHAD)

No mam, he came into the store alone, he bought a pack of cigarette's and he walked back out. that's all I know mam. (nodded no, answer he calm.)

(CONT REYNOLDS)

Mr. TAYLOR, did you notice a car leaving in a hurry, or someone walking down the street or across the street, anyone at all?(asked her sensible?)

(CONT CHAD)

(He wipe's sweat from his forehead and face with a rag) Lady, like I said, I did not see or hear anything at all, or any car leaving. Now mam, if you do not mind, it's time I get started locking up for the night. (answer he a little calmer)

(DIALOGUE)

(She hands him one of her card)

Mr. TAYLOR, if you think of anything at all, will you please give me a call?

(asked her, as CHAD nodded yes.)

(CONT CHAD)

I have no problem with that. (answer he.)

(DIALOGUE)

(MICHELLE walked out.)

As REYNOLDS reached STEIN and officer's PETE and ROY standing by his squad car, while other uniform officer's were continuing canvassing the area.

(STEIN)

MICHELLE, what did you find Out from the store clerk?

(asked he serious?)

(REYNOLDS)

(She looked disappointed)

(CONT REYNOLDS)

The store clerk claim's he did not hear anything or see anyone when he were inside or when he came out to throw away his trash. (said her looking at him.)

(CONT STEIN)

MICHELLE, look how close that car is parked at the store door. (She look's) Now you mean to tell me, that guy could not hear a gun shot Inside that store, that close? (asked he a little ferocious?)

(CONT REYNOLDS)

That's what he said, and there is something else STEVE, He seemed to be a little scared, now being nervous is one thing, when you find someone shot. But when someone are a little scared, that maybe something else, like someone would be coming after him for talking to much to the police. He also were very reliable with the information he did have. (said her, nodded yes.)

(CONT REYNOLDS)

PETE, what have the canvas turn up, if anything at all?

(asked her?)

(PETE)

(look's around and at her.)

So far, nothing yet(nodded no)nothing at all.

(answer he.)

(CONT STEIN)

MICHELLE, let's see what AIL have.

(said he.)

(DIALOGUE)

They all walked over to where AIL were kneeling down over the body.

(CONT STEIN)

AIL, what do you know, now about this guy?

(asked he?)

(AIL)

(He stood up looking at them.)

This guy die instantly, I'm sorry to say, he took two in the chest at a very close range. (He open a plastic bag and take's out a wallet, he open it.) His name is BRYANT WINSLOW. (He looked straight at them.) You know, if he would have live another month he would have turned twenty one year old. He die around 10'51 or 10'55PM tonight right here were he lay's(He pointed) The scum who ever it is, responsible for these killing's. If you people don't hurry up and catch this scum soon, someone just maybe investigating my death or yours.

(said he serious nodded toward them.)

(DIALOGUE)

As AIL and another forensic started preparing the body for transportation to EMILY for Autopsy. The rest of them walked away slow.)

(CONT STEIN)

PETE you and ROY find out from the other's if they have anything from canvassing alright. (said he looking at them.)

(CONT REYNOLDS)

(looked at him.)

You know STEVE, this do not make any sense at all to me. first I were a little depress, but now I'm just about going crazy because we can not find an eye witness or a liability person that have some intelligent information about these damn killing's. (said her frustrate.)

(DIALOGUE)

Officer's PETE and ROY and the other's police, found nothing from canvassing so they all left.

(DIALOGUE)

The next morning REYNOLDS and STEIN decided, STEIN will go to EMILY Autopsy room checking for any evidence that may lead them to a suspect concerning this murder. In the mean time REYNOLDS went to records to do a back ground check on BRYANT WINSLOW.

(CONT)

As STEIN entering the Autopsy room, EMILY seated at a table looking through a microscope. BRYANT on a table with a sheet over him,

(STEIN)

Morning EMILY. (said he smile)

(EMILY look's up at him)

(EMILY)

O good morning STEVE. (answer her smile)

(CONT STEIN)

EMILY I know you are a busy girl, and I sure don't want you to think I'm just being a hypocrite as well.

(CONT STEIN)

But seriously EMILY, what can you tell me about Mr. WINSLOW death? (asked he serious?)

(EMILY)

Excuse me a minute. (She walked over to her desk, and pick's up a file, and walked over to the table, standing by BRYANT)

(CONT EMILY)

(She open the file.)

STEVE, not a hold lot at this point. I hope to have a full complete autopsy report by noon today.

(answer her respectfully.)

(CONT STEIN)

(He look's at the body)

EMILY,(Nodded yes) I'm sure the gun shot's took this guy out.

(said he, looking at her.)

(CONT EMILY)

(She close the file. holding it against her chest.) You'll right STEVE, two shot's straight through the heart, the same as the last victim I ran an autopsy on. And STEVE this guy here also had a lot of gun powder on his clothes, that also tell me he were shot at close range, STEVE, what I already know is the M.O. from last week are the exactly the same as this one here, one bullet follower the other into the body, piercing the heart twice. This is very unusual to see two week apart. (Nodded toward him, said her professional)

(CONT STEIN)

These guy's knew their assassin, but who, why?

(asked he with a straight face?)

(CONT)

EMILY walked back to the table, where the microscope were and having a seat at it.

(CONT EMILY)

I can't answer that STEVE. (answer her looking into the microscope.)

(CONT STEIN)

(Nodded yes)

Thank's a lot EMILY,

(said he.)

(DIALOGUE)

(STEVE leave's.)

(DIALOGUE)

In the mean time REYNOLDS went to records to do a back ground check on BRYANT WINSLOW. She found out that BRYANT were recently Arrested with DALLAS JAMES and

ERNEST WESLEY for bank robbery, and made bail. with no hesitation she went straight to STEIN, where he were sitting at his desk talking on the phone.

(She approached his desk a little fast)

(REYNOLDS)

STEVE, you need to hang up right now, look what I found on the dead guy from last night, (said her with a polite attitude.)

(STEIN hang's up the phone, she give's him a file.)

(STEIN)

(He stand's up, open the file)

So MICHELLE, the guy that were kill last week, and this guy last night—knew each other. MICHELLE, not only these guy's were humiliated and left on the street dead. I think they were just point blank murder. But for what reason?

(asked he, with the expression of care, looking at her?)

(CONT REYNOLDS)

(Nodded her head yes.)

Yeah STEVE, I'LL agree with you there. This also explain this situation a little better, someone really wanted these guy's dead. The question now is by who and why?

(asked her very sensible, looking at him?)

(CONT STEIN)

(He look's at the next page.)

MICHELLE, there is a third name here, his name is DALLAS JAMES, he live at 214 pin oak dr. MICHELLE, maybe we better get there as fast as we can, and have a conversation with him. Because he may have some information about all of this killing's, and he just may need some protection as well from who ever is responsible for these murder's.

(said he very concern, looking at her.)

(DIALOGUE)

As REYNOLDS, turned around to leave, STEIN grab his jacket off his chair and they walked out and enter their car. And went to the JAMES home.

NEW-SCENE (DIALOGUE)
SLUG-LINE-SAME-MORNING-THE JAMES-HOME
CHARCATER-FATHER-MELVIN JAMES-AFRICAN-AMERICAN-TALL
CHARCATER-MOTHER-ALICE JAMES-AFRICAN-AMERICAN-MEDIUM-TALL
CHARCATER-SISTER-TONYA JAMES-AFRICAN-AMERICAN-MEDIUM-TALL

(CONT DIALOGUE)

After they exited out of their car and climbing the step's, STEIN knocked on the front door. The door open with DALLAS standing there with only blue jean pant's and black tennis shoe on, no shirt on, muscle built.

(STEIN)

Sir I'm detective STEIN and this is my partner, detective REYNOLDS. Could we talk to you for a few minute's sir? (said and asked he, with a serious voice?)

(DALLAS)

I guess so, but what is this about? (answer he, with a surprise face.)

(CONT STEIN)

Sir, would you mind, if we come in for a minute?
(asked he?)

(DIALOGUE)

(DALLAS step's back, they enter the house, see's his sister TONYA seated at a table in the back ground.)

(REYNOLDS)

Sir, do you know a Mr. DALLAS JAMES? (asked her, looking at DALLAS)

(CONT DALLAS)

Yes, that's me, why?

(answer he, with a straight face.)

(CONT STEIN)

Sir, would you mind showing some I.D.?

(asked he?)

(DALLAS showed his driver license.)

(CONT STEIN)

Mr. JAMES, how well did you know a Mr. BRYANT WINSLOW, and a Mr. ERNEST WESLEY?

(asked he with a serious attitude?)

(CONT DALLAS)

We were like three brother's from our child hood, until ERNEST were shot to death for no reason.

(answer he, sincere seriously.)

(CONT REYNOLDS)

We understand all three of you were recently arrested for bank robbery? When were the last time you saw Mr. BRYANT WINSLOW? (asked her with a straight face, looking at him?)

(CONT DALLAS)

Why are you-all asking me about BRYANT? I saw him last week paying our respect's at ERNEST parents house, and at ERNEST funeral. We just made a stupid mistake, robbing that bank.

We had no money or job, we could not find work no where at all. It were just a stupid mistake on our part. And I have not been comfortable with myself since one of my best friend have die.
(answer he, with sincere sad frustration.)

(CONT STEIN)
Were anyone of you, into drugs or anything illegal at all? or were you having any trouble with someone else? Did you see BRYANT last night,
(asked he serious?)

(CONT DALLAS)
(He take's a deep Breath with both hands on his waste.) Alright sir, I saw BRYANT around 7'PM last night at his parents house. And no we were not into drugs or anything illegal at all. And no we were not in any trouble with anyone else either. robbing that bank were the very first time we ever broke the law, and now ERNEST is dead and now BRYANT and I will stand trial alone, because of our stupid decision and behavior, breaking the law Have you-all found ERNEST killer yet?
(answer and asked he in a loud voice, with a straight face.)

(CONT REYNOLDS)
(She take's a step toward him, putting her left hand on his right shoulder.)
Mr. JAMES, we are very sorry to inform you that Mr. BRYANT WINSLOW were murder last night outside a store. Do you know anything at all about that?
(said and asked her, with a sincere expression of sensitive passion)

(CONT DALLAS)
(Soft tear's down his face, shaking his head no.) O no, no,(crying he, laying his head on REYNOLDS shoulder. He lifted his head.) Why, please tell me Why,(looking at REYNOLDS (asked he loud, with a very rebellious depressing Attitude.)

(DIALOGUE)

(His sister TONYA heard them and came very fast up front to them

(TONYA)

DALLAS, what is going on here? (asked her serious excited, looking at her brother?)

(CONT STEIN)

Mam, do you know a BRYANT WINSLOW?
(asked he?)

(CONT TONYA)

(looking at DALLAS and STEIN)

Yes I do, he is my brother here,(She pointed her finger) best friend, But why do you ask?

(ask her?)

(CONT REYNOLDS)

Mam, we just inform Mr. JAMES here, that Mr. BRYANT was murder last night.

(answer her.)

(CONT TONYA)

(She fold her arm's with a surprise shocking face.) BRYANT, (pause) BRYANT WINSLOW were murder last night, by who, I bet another drive by, right? (Nodded yes, asked her?)

(CONT STEIN)

We really don't know that yet mam. (said he, looking at her.)

(CONT REYNOLDS)

Mr. JAMES we are investigating both of there death now, and our investigation lead us here to you. We were hoping maybe

(CONT REYNOLDS)

you could give's us some good information or lead us to the person or person, responsible for their death, (said her, looking at him, with a remorse face.)

(DIALOGUE)

(DALLAS, had calm down some and had wiped some of his tear's away from his face.)

(CONT DALLAS)

Detective, I can not think of no one at all, wanted to hurt either one of my friends. (shaking his head no) They were real good guy's, until we made that stupid mistake, robbing that bank.

(answer he, very sad looking at them.)

(CONT STEIN)

(He give's DALLAS one of his card)

Sir, if you think of anything at all, please give me a call, and thank you sir for talking to us. But in the mean time try not to be out alone at no time at all, until we get this case solved.

(said and asked he? with passion concern.)

(CONT DALLAS)

Yes sir I will call you. (answer he respectfully.)

(DIALOGUE)

REYNOLDS and STEIN walked outside to their car. As they were leaving in their car with STEIN driving.

(CONT STEIN)

MICHELLE, that guy back there, he do not have a clue of what is really going on or why? He had no evidence at all to offer us or any direct person as a suspect to offer us as well. (A little smile) MICHELLE, did I or did I not witness you, Blushing just a little, when we were talking to DALLAS back there with no shirt on. (Nodded his head backward) (said he with a honest attitude.)

(CONT REYNOLDS)
STEVE, if you do not mine me saying so none of your business man.
(said her a little excited, looking at him.)
(STEIN, just looked out the driver window, while driving)

NEW-SCENE (DIALOGUE)
SLUG-LINE-TWO-NIGHT-LATER THE-WIN SLOW-FAMILY-HOME
CHARCATER-MOTHER-KATHLEEN WINSLOW-AFRICAN-AMERICAN-MEDIUM-TALL
CHARCATER-SISTER-NICOLE WINSLOW-AFRICAN-AMERICAN-MEDIUM-TALL
CHARCATER-YOUNGER-SISTER-AMBER WINSLOW-AFRICAN-AMERICAN-BOOT-TEE

While the WINSLOW family KATHLEEN, NICOLE, and AMBER were seated around the living room with other biological family members and friends. KATHLEEN were telling her family how depressed she felt the day before she received the word from the military that her husband ANDREW WINSLOW had been kill in IRAQ the year before. He had been in the military service for thirty seven years, and now our only son is dead. Suddenly there were knock at the front door, where NICOLE answer the knock at the door.

(NICOLE)
(She open the door.)
Hello DALLAS, come on in.
(said her, with a cold smile.)

(DALLAS)
(He enter in.)

Hello, how is everyone doing?

(asked he, looking a little stress?)

(THE ENTIRE HOUSE)

(LOOKING AT HIM)

Hello DALLAS, JUST FINE DALLAS.

(KATHLEEN)

DALLAS, I've been wanting to talk to you. come set beside me. (meaning a chair)

(DALLAS walk's over, and have a set beside her.)

(He look's at other people)

DALLAS, look at me son,(He look's) I want you to tell me everything you and BRYANT were involve with, other than robbing that bank?

(said her with a sincere attitude.)

(CONT DALLAS)

Miss KATHLEEN, robbing that bank were the only thing, BRYANT, ERNEST and myself were involve with.

(answer he seriously.)

(CONT KATHLEEN)

Are you sure you-all were not into gang activity, such as harassing innocent people for just cause?

(asked her?)

(CONT DALLAS)

(He clear his throat)

(CONT DALLAS)

Miss KATHLEEN, The only thing BRYANT, ERNEST and I were into, were robbing that bank. (Nodded yes) getting into gang's did not interest either one of us, or gang's activity. I do wish we had never broke the law, robbing that bank. I'm so sorry we did. (said he a little emotion, a little embarrass.)

(CONT NICOLE)

(Seated beside AMBER on the cough, her arms fold, looking straight at DALLAS.)

DALLAS, in the first place, why did you-all robbed that bank, and now my brother is dead, why?(She set up a little) who's idea was it?(Bobbing her head from side to side, asked her with an attitude, and a straight face?)

(Her mother looked at her.)

(CONT DALLAS)

Just being stupid NICOLE

(Nodded yes, answer he.)

(CONT KATHLEEN)

Well DALLAS, that were stupid of you-all. But you are the last one of the three of you. So what are you going to do now? (asked her direct?)

(CONT DALLAS)

Miss KATHLEEN, I really don't know myself at this time and point. ((He looked straight at her.) Miss KATHLEEN, again I'm very sorry what happen to my two best friends. Now if you all will excuse me, I really do need 'to get on home myself, (said he uncomfortable)

(CONT KATHLEEN)

(She stood up, as DALLAS walked to the front door)

DALLAS, you be real careful, going home, you hear me boy?

(said her, looking at him?)

(CONT DALLAS)

Yes mam, I will,

(answer he.)

(DIALOGUE)

(DALLAS walked out, to go home. And he never did admitted, who's idea it were to rob that bank, from the three of them.)

NEW-SCENE (DIALOGUE)
SLUG-LINE-LATE-EVENING-CHAD-STORE
INT-EXT-ONE-WEEK-LATER-SUNSHINE
CHARACTER-TWELVE YEAR OLD-CACUASIAN-BOB8Y ALLEN
CHARACTER-TWELVE YEAR OLD-CACUASIAN-TY ROSS
CHARACTER-FATHER-RUSSELL ALLEN-CACUASIAN-MEDIUM-TALL
CHARACTER-MOTHER-LOUIS ALLEN-CACUASIAN-SHORT

Later that evening BOBBY and TY got off their bicycle and enter the store. TY had money to buy drink and candy. After TY had made his choice of drink and candy, he approached the counter to pay. CHAD notice BOBBY picking up a candy bar in one of the ail's and sticking it into his sock, pulling his pants leg down over it, immediately CHAD locked the front door and call the police, police arrived in minutes and carried BOBBY, his bike and candy bar to the magistrate office down town, where his parents were call and they were told by the magistrate to appear before judge SAM MASON the next morning.

NEW-SCENE (DIALOGUE)
SLUG-LINE-NEXT-MORNING-9'AM
INT-COURT-ROOM-OTHER-PEOPLE-IN-COURT ROOM
CHARACTER-ATTORNEY-JUDY KING-CACUASIAN-MEDIUM-TALL

(MONICA BALL)

Your honor, docket number 01865, the state verse one BOBBY ALLEN. The charge is shop lifting, A candy bar from one seven eleven store. Manager by one Mr. CHAD TAYLOR. Little Mr. ALLEN are represent by one attorney JUDY KING.

(said her, in a normal voice, reading the charger.)

(She give's paper work to judge SAM MASON.)

(JUDGE)

Good morning Miss KING, how do your young client plead? (asked he, with an attitude?)

(Miss KING)

(standing with BOBBY and his parents)

Good morning judge, your honor, he is just a twelve year old kid. your honor, boys will be boys, your honor not guilty your honor.

(answer her, with a gentle smile)

(CONT JUDGE)

(He set up straight, clear his throat, looking at them.) And no one gave him the right to go out, act stupid and steal either. The fine is five hundred dollars, plus the cost of court. Mr. and Mrs. ALLEN, you better keep him away from that store. And if you do not pay this money by five o'clock today, your stupid little shop lifting brat will spend six months in a half way house, with no visitation rights from either one of you. Do you understand me?

(Shouted he in a loud strong voice.)

(RUSSELL)
(INSTANTLY)

Just a minute judge, are you sure, you are the right judge presiding over a twelve year old kid case?

(asked he, with a little frustration in his face and voice?)

(CONT JUDGE)

Sir, you need to shut your mouth right now, and let your attorney do the talking.

(said he, with an serious attitude.)
(RUSSELL got very Quite, looking at the judge.)

(CONT Miss KING)

Your honor, you can not be serious, five hundred dollars is very high for one little old candy bar, against a twelve year old child.

(answer her, very irritate.)

(CONT JUDGE)

Miss KING, if I do not try and stop him now, before we will know anything at all, he will be out there all grown up breaking the law more times then we all can count. Mr. and Mrs. ALLEN, take your little stupid brat home and you better teach him some serious manners. Now get the hell out of my court room, before I change my mind, right now all of you.

(JUDGE)
(Shouted he angry, with no respect to anyone.)

(DIALOGUE)
(They all left the court room, shaking their heads, in shame.)
The ALLEN'S did pay the money's that day.)

NEW-SCENE (DIALOGUE)
SLUG-LINE-ONE-MONTH-LATER
EXT-MID-NIGHT

As DALLAS were turning in for the night at his parents house, on pin oak dr. When he were about to step on the bottom step to the sidewalk up to the house. A black mrecedes car, roll up slow, light's off, passenger car window go's down. DALLAS turned around and look's at the car, with silence gun in hand, secret justice pump's two shot's into his chest, killing him instantly, secret justice pick's up black handkerchief, wipe's barrel of gun off. Let car window up leave scene quietly.

NEW-SCENE (DIALOGUE)
SLUG-LINE
NEXT-MORNING-6'AM
THE-JAMES-HOME

As DALLAS sister TONYA came out the house that morning for work, she found her brother (DALLAS) on the front step's dead. instantly running back inside, she call out to her parents MELVIN and ALICE JAMES and call the police.

(CONT DIALOGUE)

With in minute's police arrived with forensic AIL, REYNOLDS and STEIN on the scene, with the JAMES family inside the house, very sad. As uniform police were putting up yellow crime tape around the scene, REYNOLDS talked to forensic AIL.

(REYNOLDS)

How long has it been since this shooting happen AIL?
(asked her seriously, looking at him?)

(AIL)

It look's to be sometime around midnight.
(answer he sincere.)

(REYNOLDS)
(with a very surprise face)

He's been laying out here all that time, and no one notice him a passing car or someone walking down the sidewalk. Let me go in here, and have a talk with his family.

(DIALOGUE)

Come on STEVE. said her looking at him. As REYNOLDS and STEIN enter the house, with officer ROY with the family, TONYA approached REYNOLDS and STEIN. They showed their badges.

(REYNOLDS)

Hi I'm detective REYNOLDS and this is my partner, detective STEIN. Do you remember us?
(asked her serious, looking at TONYA?)

(TONYA)
(She wiped her eye's, nodded yes)
Yes I do remember you.
(answer her with sadness.)

(CONT REYNOLDS)

Mam, what is your name again? (asked her sincere?)

(TONYA)

My name is TONYA JAMES. That's my brother DALLAS on the step's dead out there, (answer her sad.)

(STEIN)
(Nodded yes)

Yes, we remember now, and we are very sorry for your lost. But can we talk to you about what happen here?
(asked he polite?)

(TONYA)

We don't know, (Nodded no) we did not hear or see anything at all last night.

(answer her sincere.)

(STEIN)

About what time, everyone were in for the night here, Excusing DALLAS, and came out this morning?

(asked he serious?)

(CONT TONYA)

I got home around 10'30PM last night. My parents, they were here watching T.V. No one (nodded no) never knows where DALLAS is until he comes home. I were in bed around 11'30PM, as well as my parents. This morning I open the front door around 6'AM to go to work, and there was DALLAS on the front step's dead.

(answer her with deep sorrow, of soft tears.)

(CONT REYNOLDS)

Do you or your parents know, if he were having any problem's or trouble with anyone?

(asked her serious?)

(CONT TONYA)

No I don't know,

(answer her, nodded her head no.)

(CONT STEIN)

May we speak to your parents?
(asked he with a straight face?)

(DIALOGUE)

TONYA turned her head a little, and call out to her parents. They both came up front.

(CONT STEIN)

Mr. and Mrs. JAMES, I'm detective STEIN(shaking hands with both of them.) and this is my partner detective REYNOLDS. Sir, what can you tell us about your son DALLAS?

(asked he serious)

(MELVIN)

What can I tell you, my son is dead, that what. (nodded yes) (answer he in a loud voice and serious face.)

(CONT REYNOLDS)

Sir, what we mean is, do you know if he were involve with anything illegal or if anyone that you know of had made any serious threat's against him?

(CONT REYNOLDS)

(asked her with a straight face.)

(MELVIN)

(Both hands on his waste)

Let me tell yall something. I know for a fact my son were not into anything illega1 (nodded his head) such as drug's. and by DALLAS been as strong as he were, if anyone made a threat against him, and we here knowing the way he were, that person would have to prove that threat to him right then on the spot, no question ask.

(answer he in a strong voice, and straight face)

(STEIN looked at ALICE)

(CONT STEIN)

Mrs. JAMES, do you know of anything at all about your son, such as who did he spend a lot of time with? (asked he polite?)

(ALICE)

BRYANT and ERNEST are the only one's, I know he hang around with, (answer her honestly.)

(CONT STEIN)

Did he have a girlfriend or were he mess around with someone else girlfriend or wife?

(asked he sincere?)

(CONT TONYA)

ALL I know is, there is someone name SHIRLEY. I don't know who she is or where she live,(nodded no) that's all I know I don't know no more then that.

(answer her with a wise attitude.)

(DIALOGUE)

REYNOLDS take's out one of her cards and give's it to ALICE. The phone ring and ALICE leave's to answer it.

(MELVIN)

(pointing his first finger)

Detective, I don't give a damn who every it is responsible for killing my son. (He looked straight at them.) But I'm telling you this, you better get in a hurry and find this person.

(said he in a strong voice, and angry face.)

(CONT STEIN)

(Taking a step toward MELVIN, putting one hand on his shoulder.) Mr. JAMES, with all do respect to you and your family, please do not take the law into your own hands. (nodded no.) please sir let the law handle this.

(said he serious.)

(DIALOGUE)

(STEIN and REYNOLDS walked out and leave the scene) IN their car.

NEW-SCENE-CARRBORO-N.C. (DIALOGUE)
SLUG-LINE-TWO-MONTH-LATER-FALL-OF-YEAR
INT-EXT-SATURDAY-MORNING-10'AM-PI-NE-STREET
CHARACTER-DAUGHTER-DEBBIE-FREEMAN-CAUCASIAN-TWELVE-YEARS-OLD
CHARACTER-MOTHER-DOROTHY-FREEMAN-CAUCASIAN-MEDIUM-TALL
CHARACTER-RUSTY SHAW-CAUCASIAN-MEDIUM-TALL-CHEEK-STREET
CHARACTER-NIEGHBOR-BETTY-WHEELER-CAUCASIAN-MEDIUM-TALL

(DIALOGUE)

A unregister silent sexual molester predator in the community. DEBBIE with her mother DOROTHY exit out of their house. As DEBBIE get's ready to get on her bicycle to go to her grandparents house as usual on a Saturday morning, one street over. Oak street. Thirty five year old RUSTY SHAW, set in his red pick up truck, parked down the street from the FREEMAN house. While their neighbor BETTY were getting grocery out of her car, across the street. DOROTHY and BETTY wave to each other. DEBBIE and her mother say's good-by, DOROTHY enter back into the house,, while DEBBIE ride down the sidewalk. As DEBBIE approached the truck, with RUSTY standing on the sidewalk on the passenger side of his truck, instantly he grab her off the bike. With a little scream, instantly he put duck tape over her mouth and risk and put her into his truck and drive away, leaving the bike behind. As BETTY witness the kidnapping, in a loud voice, she call out to DOROTHY, and with her cell phone, she dial 911. With in minutes, police officer PETE arrived on the scene. As DOROTHY and BETTY very nervous standing on the sidewalk, officer PETE exit out of his police car.

(PETE)
What happen here?
(asked he serious?)

(BETTY)

Officer, I just witness this women little girl, being kidnapped down the street.

(answer her very excited.)

(He look's at DOROTHY)

(CONT PETE)

Oh yeah, by who?

(asked he, straight face?)

(DOROTHY)

I don't know officer, I were in my house, BETTY here saw it all, I don't know, I just don't know.

(answer her crying, shaking her head no.)

(He look's at BETTY)

(CONT PETE)

Just what did you see or witness mam?

(asked he?)

(CONT BETTY)

Officer, I heard DEBBIE scream, then I saw a white guy, put tape over her mouth and risk, and then he put her in a red pick up truck and drive away.

(answer her, excited concern.)

(CONT PETE)

Do anyone of you, know who (asked he sincere?) this person is?

(CONT BETTY)

Nodded no, I don't know, who he is. (answer her sensitive.)

(BETTY look's at DOROTHY)

(CONT DOROTHY)

I have no idea who he is, or why this man did this.

(answer her with a emotionally voice.)

(CONT PETE)

Excuse me, I need to call this in, and get a canvas started.
(said he with an officer expression.)

(DIALOGUE)

PETE call it in. In minute's other uniform police officer's arrived on the scene, to start canvassing the area. After PETE gave the information about the red truck to other officer's, they all leave to canvas the area. PETE looked back at BETTY.

(CONT PETE)

BETTY, did you get a good look at this guy? or can you give's us a good description of this person?
(asked he with a straight face?)

(CONT BETTY)

I did not get a real good look at his face. He were about my height, with blue jean's on and a blue shirt, with a black baseball cap on.

(answer her still sensitive.)

(CONT PETE)

Thank you very much. (answer he polite.)

(DIALOGUE)

(PETE enter his car, and leave the scene.)

NEW-SCENE—(DIALOGUE)
SLUG-LINE THE-SAME-MORNING
CHARACTER-GRANDMOTHER-VIRGINA__-
FREEMAN-CAUCASIAN-SHORT CHARACTER-A
FRIEND-CHARLIE-RODGERS-CAUCASIAN-TWELVE-
YEARS-OLD

(DIALOGUE)

As DOROTHY had stop crying and enter back into her house, BETTY returned back to her car to finish with her grocery from her car into her house. Other neighbors came out of their home's with wondering mind's. As DOROTHY were talking on the phone to her mother, VIRGINA FREEMAN. There were a sudden knock at her front door, by one of DEBBIE little friend name CHARLIE RODGERS. DOROTHY answer the door.

(DOROTHY)

Hi CHARLIE, come on in. (said her serious.)

(CHARLIE go's in)

(DOROTHY walk's over and pick's up the phone.)

(CONT DOROTHY)

Mom, I don't know why this man grab DEBBIE and took her away like he did. The police is looking for him right now.

(CONT DOROTHY)

(said her very irritate excited.)

(VIRGINA)

Honey, do you think this man maybe a sexual molester, or something else?

(asked her very concern seriously?)

(CONT DOROTHY)

Mom, I don't know what to think, I'm already starting to go crazy, it's no telling what this man maybe doing to my child.

(said her, soft tears down her face.)

(VIRGINA)

DOROTHY, I'm coming over right now. (said her with passion.)

(DIALOGUE)

They hang up. DOROTHY wipe's her eye's with a white handkerchief, and look's at CHARLIE standing by the front door.

(CHARLIE)

Hi Miss DOROTHY, is DEBBIE here? (said and asked he?)

(CONT DOROTHY)

CHARLIE, have you Heard anything about DEBBIE this morning?

(asked her, serious, looking at him?)

(CONT CHARLIE)

heard what? No I have not heard anything at all about DEBBIE. What about DEBBIE, Miss DOROTHY?

(answer he, a little surprise.)

(CONT DOROTHY)

(CHARLIE sit down. (They have a seat on the couch) CHARLIE, there is a possible chance DEBBIE were kidnapped this morning, right down the street by someone driving a red truck. Do you know of anyone, who drive such a truck?

(asked her serious, looking at him?)

(CONT CHARLIE)

(He pause a moment)

Miss DOROTHY, there is a truck like that be park down the street from my house on cheek street.

(instantly said he, excited irritate.)

(CONT DOROTHY)

O yeah, would you mind talking to the police about that CHARLIE?

(asked her, excited?)

(CONT CHARLIE)

No mam, I sure don't.

(answer he.)

(DOROTHY get's up and walked over to the phone.)

(CONT DOROTHY)

Let me call the police back here so you can talk to them, Is that alright with you CHARLIE?

(asked her, looking at him?)

(CONT CHARLIE)

Nodded yes, yes mam.

(answer he.)

(DIALOGUE)

After DOROTHY, made the call. She waits by the front door open. With in minutes officer PETE returns at her house he exit out of his car and enter the house. CHARLIE stands up.

(CONT DOROTHY)

Officer CROCKER, this is one of my daughters friend, his name is CHARLIE RODGERS. He may have some helpful information concerning my daughters disappearance. will you please listen to what he have to say?

(said and asked her very excited?)

(PETE look's at CHARLIE)

What can you tell me son, about this situation?

(asked he serious?)

(CONT CHARLIE)

After Miss DOROTHY, told me, what happen to DEBBIE. I know there is such a truck, be park down the street, from where I live. and sometime's be park by the back door at his house. and the man that drive's that truck, always wear's a black baseball cap.

(answer he sensible.)

(CONT PETE)

And where do you live CHARLIE?

(asked he, straight face?)

(CONT CHARLIE)

(He pointed his left finger to his left) Two street's over that way on cheek street.

(answer he.)

(DIALOGUE)

As PETE, CHARLIE, and DOROTHY steps out onto the front porch. PETE get's on his radio, alerting other officer's to watch for such red truck on cheek street. CHARLIE go's down the street get's DEBBIE bike and return to the house. PETE look's at him.

(CONT PETE)

CHARLIE, will you be willing to ride with me, and show me just where this person live?

(asked he sensitive polite?)

(CONT CHARLIE)

(He pause)

No I don't mine, But am I in any trouble (asked he, polite?)

(CONT PETE)

(He put one of his hand on CHARLIE shoulder)

No son, you are not in any trouble at all. Just show me where this person live.

(answer he with a honest decent attitude.)

(CONT DOROTHY)

Officer PETE I have live here on pine street most of my life. This is the first time something like this has happen here, especial involving my child, right in the front door of my house, please find my child, please sir. (said her, a little emotion, looking at PETE.)

(CONT PETE)

Miss FREEMAN, we will do the best we can. I promise you that.

(answer he straight face.)

NEW-SCENE (DIALOGUE)
SLUG-LINE-SAME-MORNING

As CHARLIE showed officer PETE, where RUSTY live, with other officer in the area, they quickly surrounded the house. with RUSTY truck parked at the back door. PETE told CHARLIE to stay in the car, as he exit out. PETE knock's on the front door, with RUSTY answer it with no shirt on, just pants and a little sweaty.

(RUSTY)

Yeah, just what the hell do you want?

(asked he with a real nasty attitude?)

(CONT PETE)

Sir, I need to talk to you for a moment. Will you please step out for a second, please sir?

(answer and asked he very serious?)

(DIALOGUE)

RUSTY step's out onto the front porch, instantly the police heard a norse from inside the back of the house. PETE grab RUSTY, pulling him off the porch down to the ground. Other police on top of RUSTY, while PETE with two other police officer's rushed into the house. They found DEBBIE in a back bedroom, on the bed, handcuff to the bed with duck tape over her mouth, nude waste down. unhurt, But very nervously scared. Instantly RUSTY SHAW were arrested for first degree kidnapping and first degree rape. and were carried to jail.

NEW-SGENE (DIALOGUE)
SLUG-LINE-MONDAY-MORNING-9'15AM'
INT-COURT-ROOM-ARRANGMENT
CHARACTER-ATTORNEY-WILLIAM-WILCOX-
CAUCASIAN-SHORT-MAN
COURT-ROOM-FULL-OF-PEOPLE

(MONICA BALL)

Your honor, docket number 99027. The state of north Carolina verse one RUSTY SHAW. The charge is kidnapping in the first degree, rape in the first degrees of one twelve year old child. As she give's paper work to judge SAM MASON, she look' at RUSTY SHAW with an attitude.

(JUDGE MASON)

Mr. WILCOX, with all due respect to you, I need a plead right now.

(said he, a strong attitude.)

(ATTORNEY WILCOX)

Not guilty your honor, with a Biological mental explanation.

(answer he, responsible normal voice.)

(CONT JUDGE)

Well, you can just save your biological explanation for the trial judge.

(said he, strong voice.)

(Judge look's at the D.A.)

(CONT JUDGE)

Mr. FUTCH, if you please, application for bail?

(said he polite.)

(FUTCH)

Your honor, due to the liability of this defendant dangerous reputation in our society. He must face all consequences, with his aggravated assault on the general public. especial around children. Judge the state is requesting two million dollars on bail. If you can respect it this time judge.

(answer he calm voice.)

(CONT WILCOX)

Your honor, my client and I do not appreciate the expression the D.A. is giving us here today. We are not just a right down suspicion fool either. Two million dollars is much too high.

(instantly said he with a attitude.)

(CONT JUDGE)

Mr. WILCOX, The D.A. did not break the constitutional of the law either. Your client will face all obligation concerning these charge's. I'm also giving you and your client, a warning. If he need psychiatrist treatment or help, he better get in a hurry and get it. and he better be well prepared for trial with the acceptance of the court's. There is no excuse being the scum of the earth. Bail is set at twenty five thousand dollars, cash or bond next case.

(said he, tap his gavel strong voice and attitude.)

(CONT FUTCH)

Judge, you are the one need psychiatrist help. This man is a very dangerous sexual molester predator, to the public. and with such low bail, you are giving him the right to go out kidnap and rape someone else child. why judge, tell me why, answer me judge.

(instantly shouted he angry.)

(CONT JUDGE)

Mr. FUTCH, I'm holding you in contempt, you are total, I mean completely out of order this time. you are going to jail for the next twelve hour's. (judge look's at sheriff GEORGE) sheriff Take Mr. FUTCH into custody, and slap the damn handcuff on him, hurry up, get him out of my sight. (said he with rage)

(DIALOGUE)

As sheriff GEORGE cuffed and carried Mr. FUTCH to jail. He were release from jail at 9'30'PM that night. RUSTY SHAW posted bail that Monday morning and were release.

NEW-SCENE—(DIALOGUE)
SLUG-LINE
INT-EXT-FRIDAY-NIGHT-OF-THAT-WEEK
RUSTY-HOUSE-1'30'AM

(CONT DIALOGUE)

RUSTY parked his truck by the back door of his house. Very intoxicate, as he begins to exit out, he sit there with the door open, motor turn off, eye's close. A black Mercedes car pull's up at the end of drive way on the street, light's off, secret justice exit out of car, leaving motor running, dog bark down the street. with ski mass on, black glove's on both hand's silence on barrel of 9mm gun, walk's up to truck open door quietly, notice how heavy intoxicate RUSTY were, secret justice pump's three shot's into RUSTY chest at close range, killing him instantly. take's out black handkerchief, wipe's barrel of gun off, walk's back to car, enter car, leave scene quietly.

NEW-SCENE (DIALOGUE)
EXT-SLUG-LINE-NEXT-MORNING-8'30'AM
CHARACTER-NEIGHBOR-ROBERT-EUBANKS-CAUCASIAN-MEDIUM-TALL

As a neighbor across the street were about to enter his car, name ROBERT EUBANKS. He notice RUSTY just sitting in his truck not moving across the street. He walk's up the drive way, calling out to him, as RUSTY cell phone were steady ringing. As he approached the truck door, he finds RUSTY dead. Instantly using his cell, he dial 911. (ROBERT waits) With in minute's forensic AIL, REYNOLDS and detective STEIN with other police officer's arrived on the scene. immediately uniform officer's started putting yellow crime tape around the scene, and started canvassing the area As forensic AIL, standing at the truck door examining the body, up walked REYNOLDS and STEIN.

(REYNOLDS)

AIL, what do you know right now about this killing?

(asked her direct serious?)

(AIL)

What I know now is, this man were murder right here where he sit's that's what I know.

(answer he with an attitude.)

(CONT REYNOLDS)

What I mean AIL, the time of death? What type of weapon were use on this man?

(said her a little frustrate?)

(CONT AIL)

MICHELLE, I just arrived here about three minute's before you-all did. if you will give me a few more minute's I just may have a description on time of death, (answer he, a little loud angry.)

(CONT REYNOLDS)

Excuse me AIL, (pointing her finger at him) I dare you take that tone of voice with me. from now on when I ask you question you better give me a straight answer. Are we clear on that? (said her loud, bobbing her head side to side.)

(STEIN)

MICHELLE, come on(holding her by her right arm walking away) MICHELLE, let AIL. do his job. and why are you expecting AIL to have a time of death on the spot?

(said and asked he, looking at her polite?)

(CONT REYNOLDS)

Alright STEVE, maybe I'm getting a little impatience wanting to catch (she take's a deep Breath) this person or person responsible for these killing's. (she looked at PETE) Who's that guy with PETE?

(said and asked her, calm.)

(CONT STEIN)

I think he's the guy call this in. Let's go have a talk with him. (said he.)

(They walked over to ROBERT and PETE.)

(They showed their badge's)

(CONT REYNOLDS)

Morning sir, I'm detective REYNOLDS and this is my partner detective STEIN. What is your name sir? and do you live here?

(said and asked her with a serious voice and face?)

(ROBERT)

My name is ROBERT EUBANKS,(nodding no) and no I do not live here. I live across the street.

(He pointing)

(answer he a little nervous.)

(STEIN)

Just what do you know, what happen here sir?

(asked he with direct passion?)

(CONT ROBERT)

I came out to go to the grocery store a few minutes ago, and I notice RUSTY just sitting in his truck, with his cell phone ringing and his door were open. I knew something were wrong, because it's not like RUSTY to be outside like this, just sitting in his truck.

(answer he polite.)

(CONT REYNOLDS)

Did you see or hear anything at all unusual last night or early this morning, before you came out? (asked her very intelligent?)

(CONT ROBERT)

No I did not. last night I were in the shower around 12'30, and no I did not see or hear anything at all last night or early this morning either. You know detective, I have live on cheek street for five years. finding someone being murder in their own back yard, is a new experience for me.

(answer he sincere.)

(DIALOGUE)

REYNOLDS notice forensic AIL. excuse me asked her? she walked over to him.

(CONT REYNOLDS)

AIL, about how long ago the decrease left this world and all of us?

(asked her seriously calm?)

(CONT AIL)

According to his body temperature and lost of blood, sometime after midnight. He took three in the chest, at a very close range.

(answer he, expression of concern.)

(CONT REYNOLDS)

Are you telling me, some crazy fool or person, just walked up here and murder this man. or just waiting for him here. I wonder what were their motive. (nodded no) I just do not understand it.

(said and asked her, with trouble eyes, and Affection)

(CONT AIL)

I guess so MICHELLE, and who ever it was, they also made sure he spend one last night in his truck. MICHELLE, why don't you find out from your other officer's, if they found anything from canvassing the area? (said and asked he, concern.)

(CONT REYNOLDS)

Thanks AIL, you are right.

(answer her serious.)

(DIALOGUE)

(She walks away to STEIN. excuse me, asked her, REYNOLDS and STEIN walk's away from ROBERT.)

(CONT REYNOLDS)

STEVE, it's about the same M.O. as in the pass. But this guy here, he took three in the chest at a close range.

Have any officer's found out anything from canvassing the area yet?

(CONT REYNOLDS)

(said and asked her sincere concern. ?)

(DIALOGUE)

(STEIN and REYNOLDS, notice officer PETE coming toward them.)

(CONT STEIN)

Hey PETE, have yall found out anything yet? (asked he sensible?)

(PETE)

(Nodded no) No, not one thing at all, and no witness either. you know, we arrested this guy, just last week-end for rape, and now he is dead. Let me see if the criminology found any finger prints yet, or something.

(answer he serious.)

(DIALOGUE)

(They all walked over to criminology TERSA)

(CONT PETE)

TERSA, have you found anything at all yet? (asked he, with a straight face?)

(TERSA)

I can not find a foot print or a finger print, not even a string of hair or any D.N.A. as well, (Nodded no) nothing at all, other then the decrease him self. This were a clean professional hit, in and out.

(answer, her responsible disappointed)

(CONT REYNOLDS)

Just that simple?(Nodded yes) I'm sure with no remorse, at all, who ever is responsible for this murder, (said and asked her serious.)

(CONT TERSA)

You got it girl, I'm going back to the lab. (answer her serious, small smile.)

(DIALOGUE)

TERSA pick up her lab criminology black equipment Box and she walk's away.

NEW-SCENE (DIALOGUE)
SLUG-LINE-THURSDAY-EVENING-5'30'PM
INT-JUDGE-SAM MASON-CHAMBER
CHARACTER-CARL LAWSON-AFRICAN-AMERI CAN-MEDIUM-TALL

Late this Thursday evening, as judge SAM MASOM were in his chamber's sitting behind his desk, reading some paper work.

There were a sudden knock at his door, by a messenger name CARL LAWSON.

(JUDGE MASON)

Come in.

(said he, strong voice.)

(CARL go's in.)

(CARL)

Are you judge SAM MASON?

(asked he normal voice, smiling?)

(CONT JUDGE)

YES I'm, why? answer he polite look's at him.

(CONT CARL)

Judge I have a subpoena for you to appear before the federal jurisdiction congressional committee on the 10th of next month, in Raleigh N.C.

(said he.)

(DIALOGUE)

(He give's the subpoena to the judge and leave's the scene.)

NEW-SCENE (DIALOGUE)
SLUG-LINE-ONE-MONTH-LATER
INT-FEDERAL-CONGRESSION-METTING A-PALING-OF-FEDERAL-JUDGE'S
RALEIGH N.C.
CHARACTER-JUDGE-HARRY WADE-CAUCASIAN-MEDIUM-TALL CHARACTER-ATTORNEY-MARGARET CUNNINGHAM-CAUCASIAN-MEDIUM-TALL

(DIALOGUE)

Standing to voice and express his appending and concern, Mr. JAMES FUTCH. judge MASON and his attorney MARGARET CUNNINGHAM are seated at a table across from him.

(MR. FUTCH)

Congress committee, I bring you here today, as the assistant district attorney of orange county, judge SAM MASON. On how judge MASON has being Miss representative the constitutional of the law. By giving some of the hard cold criminal some of the low's bail's. And when I tried to question him about it, in a court of law, he become's very angry and hypocrites to the tax payer in orange county and me. And he once threw me in jail for question his judgment call. I think judge SAM MASON owe this committee and the public an serious explanation, why he will allow first degree murder's and rape's back into our society, before they are due process in a court of law for such low bail's. Thank you.

(said he, expression of serious conversation)

(He have a seat)

(MARGARET stand's in front of the committee.)

(MARGARET)

Committees anyone can see how Mr. FUTCH, he's trying to make my client to be deception to Miss lead you and the public. As judge MASON attorney for many year's. I find this man to be very respectful to the contitutiona1 of the law. And as a judge his self, it is his just duty to make a judgment call if he thinks' a bail is too high or too low, in line with the constitutional. If we allowed Mr. FUTCH to get away with this, by changing the constitutional of our judicial systems. Then what kind of a constitutional would we have? Thank you.

(said her, with serious concern.)

(She have seat)

(CONT FUTCH)

Committee, I have been in court with this man, time and time again. And I have watched his conduct change over and over again It seems he have no care or any safety for the public or for } any defendant. Just last month a man were charge with rapping a little twelve year old girl. And one week later, that man were murder in his own truck, right in his back yard. Committee the people are asking that sanction be surrendered upon judge SAM MASON. To put a stop to his repeat of low bail and people turning up dead, because of his low bail, and his attitude toward the tax payer. Thank you.

(said he, a little excited.)

(He have a seat)

(CONT MARGARET STANDING)

Committee, Mr. FUTCH has no right to judge my client professional duty as a judge on the bench. We need to ask our self a serious question. And that is if we did not have a fare judge as my client on the bench. Then what kind of judicial systems and society and world would we all would be living in. Thank you.

(said her, very seriously.)

(She have a seat)

(senior chief JUDGE WADE)

We thank you both for your statement and testimony here today We will stand in reassess for thirty minutes upon our return and decision.

(The committee walked out.)

(DIALOGUE)
(Committee returned in thirty minutes.)

(CONT JUDGE WADE)
Mrs. CUNNINGHAM, and Mr. FUTCH, we the committee here we really do appreciate you-all statement and testimony here today. we have taking all statement and testimony here today in the deep's considerable respect under the constitutional with no president to either party, again we thank you. In this case under the law all judge's on the bench have all kind of bail to go by under the constitutional concerning the charge of all kind's of crime. If a judge thinks' he or she need to make a judgment call concerning bail is too high or too low, then they are only doing what they feel is fare and just under the constitutional of the law. Now the committee here, we thinks' that judge SAM MASON has been fare making such judgment call, we stand's agree.
(said he, fairly seriously.) (HE TAP HIS GAVEL)

(DIALOGUE)
(The committee paling of judge's walked out, and so did everyone else, with Mr. FUTCH deeply disappointed with embarrassment on his face.)

NEW-SCENE (DIALOGUE)
SLUG-LINE-THREE-MONTH-LATER
INT-EXT-BRASWELL-HOME_CHAPEL-HILL-N.C.—101-ARROWHEAD-RD
CHARACTER-SINGLE-LUTHER BRASWELL-CAUCASIAN-MEDIUM-TALL
CHARACTER-TEENAGE-DAVID HOOKER-CAUCASIAN-SHORT
CHARACTER-TEENAGE-KEVIN PATTERSON-CAUCASIAN-MEDIUM-TALL_ASHLEY CT
CHARACTER-FRANK ERWIN-CAUCASIAN-VERY-TALL

(DIALOGUE)

The A. T. F. squad received anonymous tip, that very high quality of drugs such as crack cocaine and marijuana were being sold in a very high quality education community. At a house with a fence around the yard, with three pitt guard bull dog's at night. The A.T.F, scent an under cover teenage agent in to buy drug's and to check it out DAVID HOOKER. Along with an other teenage name KEVIN PATTERSON. A high school drop out and a small time drug dealer. The number one drug dealer himself, Mr. LUTHER BRASWELL, the owner of a car dealer ship. He were always call L.B.

(DIALOGUE)

Late one Friday evening around 7'PM, KEVIN and DAVID stopped by L.B house to buy some marijuana. After KEVIN knocked on the front door, and L.B answer it. They enter the house.

(L.B.)

(smoking a cigarette)

KEVIN, who is this guy with you?

(asked he, looking direct at both of them?)

(KEVIN)

O L.B he's alright, this is one of my good friend DAVID, when I were in school. Trust me L.B (putting one of his hand on DAVID shoulder) This man is clean and alright.

(said he, with a straight face.)

(DIALOGUE)

L.B walked over to a chair and have a seat.)

(KEVIN stepped toward L.B)

(CONT KEVIN)

Hey, L.B, we want to get high tonight with some girl's, you have anything on hand now? (said and asked he, serious?)

(L.B, put his cigarette down the ash tray, and stood up.)

(CONT LB)

(POINTING HIS FIGER AT THEM) Look here KEVIN, I don't want no shit from either one of you. you understand, (Nodded his head, asked he serious?)

(CONT KEVIN)

Hey L.B, you are to know by now, we don't want no more trouble, no more then you do. (said he, nodded no.)

(CONT L.B)

Yeah, I got something, just what do yall want?

(asked he?)

(CONT KEVIN)

We are looking for some marijuana. L.B, we did not come here looking for any trouble man. just for something to get high on, that's all.

(answer he, straight face.)

(L.B. looked at DAVID)

(CONT L.B.)

That's fine, But that guy there, he's very quiet. (pointed at DAVID, DAVID smile.)

I'll be right back, how much do yall want? (said and asked he?)

(CONT KEVIN)

L.B. let us have an ounce of marijuana.

(said he.)

(DIALOGUE)

(L.B. left the room, and a few minutes later, he returned with an ounce of marijuana. They paid L.B. one hundred thirty dollars, and leave's the scene. For the next two month's either KEVIN or DAVID every week would stop by L.B house to buy drug's.

NEW-SCENE (DIALOGUE)
INT-EXT-ONE-MONTH-LATER
SLUG-LINE-L.B._-HOUSE

Early one Friday morning around 4'AM, L.B. received a large shipment of drug's. Bulk's of quantity and quality of marijuana, and cocaine. At 6'AM the next morning (SATURDAY) with a search warrant the A.T.F. squad surrounded L.B house and property line, special agent FRANK ERWIN knock's on the front door, with L.B. answer it in his pajamas. with the storm door lock, the dog's inside the house with him barking.

(AGENT ERWIN Morning sir, I have a warrant to search the house and all property premises. May we come in?

(CONT ERWIN)

(said and asked he, very serious?)

(L.B.)

Just what the hell, you people want or looking for this time of morning? it's time for me to get dress for work.

(answer he, irritated with humiliation.)

(CONT ERWIN)

Sir, are you going to let us in, or do we have to force our way in? We understands and know, you have some mean pit-bull dog's. if you want them to stay alive, you better keep them away from us, and let us do our job.

(said and asked he, straight face.)

(CONT L.B.)

wait just a minute.

(answer he.)

(DIALOGUE)

(L.B. went out back and put the dog's into another fence and return to Let the A.T.F squad in.)

(CONT L.B.)

Come on in, and don't take to long, I have a car business to run. I got to get dress.

(answer he, a little embarrass.)

(DIALOGUE)

The A.T.F, enter the house and property line, with two K9 dog's. One of the K9 dog found six kilogram of uncut cocaine, twenty five hundred pounds of marijuana, ready to be distributed to small time drug dealer's, one hundred and fifty thousand cash dollars in two card board box's, with book's on top of it, behind a piano and a long tall bookcase in the basement of the house. Instantly L.B. were arrested and carried to jail in his pajama's with his cocaine and marijuana, and cash money.

NEW-SCENE (DIALOGUE)
SLUG-LINE-MONDAY-MORN IMG-9'30'AM
CHARACTER-ATTORNEY-REBECCA PERRY-
CAUCASIAN-MEDIUM-TALL
LOT OF PEOPLE IN COURT ROOM.
INT-COURT-ARRANGEMENT

(MONICA)

Your honor, docket number G-10059-39, The state of north carolina verse one LUTHER BRASWELL. The charge is housing narcotic, trafficking narcotic, planning to distributed cocaine and marijuana, into the public. Hiding unpaid tax money from the I.R.S. in the sum of one hundred and fifty thousand cash dollars.

(said her, with a serious attitude.)
(She give's paper work to judge SAM MASON)

(JUDGE MASON)

Mrs. PERRY, do your client have any remorse of shame concerning a plead?

(asked he, with a serious attitude?)

(REBECCA)
(STANDING WITH L.B.)

With all due respect, your honor, not guilty.

(LOOKING AT THE JUDGE)
(nodded yes, answer her responsible.)

(CONT JUDGE)

Respect, she say's, well Mrs. PERRY what about your client respect for this county and community. I myself are getting a migraine, just by looking at him this morning.

(said he frustration and attitude.)

(LOOKING AT HER.)
(He look's at the D.A. Mr. FUTCH.)

(JUDGE)

Mr. FUTCH, if you please, application for bail? (asked he, attitude?)

(FUTCH, STANDING)

Judge, will it be any good, to ask for a high bail or remained?

(asked he, a little attitude?)

(LOOKING AT HIM)

(CONT JUDGE)

Mr. FUTCH, just give me a bail, right now, (shouted he, seriously.) (LOOK ING AT HIM)

(CONT FUTCH)

Alright judge, The state is requesting five million dollars, because of this defendant reputation. and he may be a flight risk, because of his hiding tax money from the I.R.S.

(answer he, seriously irritated)

(LOOKING AT HIM)

(CONT REBECCA)

Your honor, five million dollars is very much unaccepted that would put a very hardship on my client. It is not right, not right at all your honor.

(answer her instantly frustrate) (LOOK ING AT HIM)

(CONT JUDGE)

Hardship, she say's, well let's see how he is going to handle a simple migraine. Mr. BRASWELL, you are here by order to surrendered your driver license and any passport you may have at this moment.

(said he, a little loud angry, LOOKING AT HIM)

(L.B. give's driver license to REBECCA)

(CONT REBECCA)

Your honor, how will my client do for transportation? He has a car business to run. He has to get to and from work, and run different area's. And he do not have his passport right now, (said her, frustrate, LOOKING AT HIM NODDED YES)

(CONT JUDGE)

Let him hire a driver, as for we know, he may have more money hidden away from the state. Mr. LUTHER BRASWELL, you are here by order not to leave orange county or the state of north Carolina until trial, do you understand me sir?

(said and asked he? straight face, LOOKING AT HIM)

L.B.)

Yes, your honor, I do.

(answer he, responsible. LOOKING AT HIM)

(CONT JUDGE)

Good, real good, make sure you surrendered your passport real soon. Bail is set at twenty five thousand dollars, with out president, cash or bond, next case.

(said he, tap his gavel seriously, LOOKING AT HIM)

(CONT FUTCH)

Judge, why don't you just put T.V. camera's in the court room, so the hold entire county, can see how hypocrite you really are. Judge this man is responsible for putting dangerous drug's into our community and the county. Twenty five thousand dollars is much to low. Come on judge, I'm sure you can do better then that for the people of orange county.

(shouted he angry, with frustration. LOOKING AT HIM)

(CONT JUDGE)

Mr. FUTCH, twenty five thousand dollars, or else you leave it alone. And get the hell out of my court room man, right now.

(shouted he,(STANDING) with a angry face. LOOKING AT HIM)

(DIALOGUE)

Mr. FUTCH walked out of the court room very angry. L.B. made bail that morning and were release from jail.

NEW-SCENE (DIALOGUE)
SLUG-LIME-ONE-WEEK-LATER
INT-HEAD-QUARTERS_10'AM
CHARACTER-LIEUTENANT-SCOTT MACK

As REYNOLDS and STEIN were setting in her office talking together in walk's lieutenant SCOTT MACK, where he have a seat in a chair.

(SCOTT)

Ballistics, call a few minutes ago, and said they have some evidence that may interest you both. Let me insist the both of you, to get over there and find out what this is all about (said he, with decent respect. LOOKING AT THEM)

(STEIN)

Lieutenant, you mean right now? (asked he, suspicion look at SCOTT?)

(CONT SCOTT)

Yes right now, it's time we find out why is all this killing is going on and by who.

(said he, attitude. STANDING LOOKING AT THEM)

(DIALOGUE)

REYNOLDS and STEIN leave's her office for ballistics office.

NEW-SCENE (DIALOGUE)
SLUG-LINE-SAME-MORNING INT-BALLISTICS-OFFICE

As TERSA were looking into the microscope (STANDING) and talking on the phone, in walk's REYNOLDS and STEIN,

(REYNOLDS)
(SHE CLEAR HER THROAT)

Excuse me TERSA.
(said her, LOOKING AT TERSA)

(DIALOGUE)

TERSA look's up at them, and say's good-by on the phone.

(CONT REYNOLDS)

TERSA, we understand you have some evidence, you want to share with us?
(said and asked her, serious concern.)

(TERSA)

You want believe this, but I found out, all of those people were recently kill. They were kill by three different 9mm gun's. Take a look into the microscope.
(said her, sensitive polite. SHE STEP BACK)

(DIALOGUE)

(REYNOLDS and STEIN look's at three different bullet's.)
(REYNOLDS look's at TERSA.)

(CONT REYNOLDS)

So we have three different killer's on our hands?
(asked her? very excited serious, LOOKING AT HER.)

(STEIN)

That may be true MICHELLE, But how many people in orange county own a 9mm gun?

(said and asked he? expression of intelligent, LOOKING AT HER)

(CONT REYNOLDS)

I have no idea STEVE, But I think we better do some serious checking and narrow it down to these three bullet's.

(answer her respect. LOOKING AT HIM.)

(CONT TERSA, SHE FOLD HER ARM"S)

MICHELLE, how are you planning to narrow it down, by knocking on the hold county front door's?

(asked her? ABSOLUTE ACCURATE LOOKING AT HER)

(CONT REYNOLDS)

I don't know yet TERSA, But we will find away.

(nodded yes. answer her, A LITTLE CONFUSED, LOOKING AT TERSA)

(CONT STEIN)

Thanks' a lot TERSA.

(said he polite. LOOKING AT TERSA.)

(DIALOGUE)

(REYNOLDS and STEIN leave's Ballistics office.)

NEW-SCENE (DIADOGUE)
SLUG-LINE-ONE-MONTH-LATER-FRIDAY-NIGHT
EXT-1'15'AM-L.B.-HOUSE
CHARACTER-DIANE BENSON-CAUCASIAN-MEDIUM-TALL

As L.B. girlfriend DIANE were bringing him home this Friday night, in her 2004 Mazda car from a night of partying, she pull's into the driveway, To let L.B. get out. L.B. wanted her to come in But she refused. so L.B exit out of her car. As DIANE were backing out of the driveway, L.B standing there intoxicate, he wave to her. As DIANE drive down the street away from L.B house L.B open the gate from the fence and started walking slowly on the sidewalk to step's. suddenly A black Mercedes car pull's up slow, light's off and stop's in driveway. Driver car window go's down, secret justice with ski mass on, black glove's on hands, silence on barrel of 9mm gun. L.B turn around, and look's at car secret justice pump's two shot's into L.B chest, killing him instantly, L.B fall's down on the sideway dead. secret justice pick's up black handkerchief, wipe's barrel of 9mm gun off, leave's scene quietly.

NEW-SCENE (DIALOGUE)
EXT-SLUG-LINE-L.B.-HOUSE
CHARACTER-TYLER NELSON-AFRICAN-MERICAN-MEDIUM-TALL

Early that Saturday morning around 6'45'AM, as L.B, neighbor next door name Mr. TYLER NELSON were coming out of his house, to go to work, KEVIN turned into L.B driveway with his dodge ram truck and he notice L.B Laying behind the fence on the side walk with lot's of blood around him. Instantly he stop in shock he jumped out. and ran over to him, as TYLER notice him too. The dog's were in a separate fence in the back yard, barking real bad. TYLER looked over at KEVIN standing in his yard.

(TYLER)

Hey man, what's wrong with L.B.? (asked he loud, with a surprise face?)

(DIALOGUE)

(On his knee's checking L.B pulse, KEVIN turned around, LOOKING AT TYLER)

(KEVIN)

Hey man, if you don't mind, call the police, L.B been shot. I think he is dead.

(answer he loud, real nervous.)

(DIALOGUE)

Instantly TYLER enter back into his house, and dial 911. with in minutes uniform police officer's, detective REYNOLDS and STEIN, with forensic AIL arrived on the scene. As TYLER watching from his yard. Police officer's started putting up yellow crime tape around the crime scene, and started canvassing the area. REYNOLDS and STEIN talk's to KEVIN. After AIL walked over to the body and kneel down and started to examine the body, KEVIN back away. REYNOLDS call KEVIN over to her and STEIN standing in the driveway. They showed their badge's.

(REYNOLDS)

Morning sir, I'm detective REYNOLDS and this is my partner detective STEIN. what is your name sir? (asked her, very serious?) (looking at him)

(KEVIN)

My name is KEVIN PATTERSON. I'm a friend of L.B there.

(He pointed, nodding his head)

(answer he, very nervous serious.) (LOOKING AT HER)

(STEIN)

Mr. PATTERSON, do you know what happen here?

(asked he, straight face?) (LOOKING AT HIM)

(CONT KEVIN)

I pull my truck into the driveway a little while ago and there L.B were Laying there, with all that blood around him. (nodded no) I don't know what happen here or why.

(answer he, direct face.) (LOOKING AT THEM)

(CONT REYNOLDS)

Do anyone else live here with him, you know of?

(nodded yes, asked her?) (LOOKING AT HIM)

(CONT KEVIN)

Nodded no—No one else live here with L.B, other then his dog's as you can see in the back yard. what I don't understand, why would anyone wanted to hurt L.B, or yet still kill him.

(said and answer he, a little loud) (LOOKING AT THEM)

(CONT STEIN)

Sir, what were your reason for stopping by here this morning?

(asked he respectfully?) (LOOKING AT HIM)

(CONT KEVIN)

L.B lost his driving license a while back, so I comes by every morning and pick him up and take him to his car dealer ship every day.

(answer he, a little emotion.) (LOOKING AT THEM)

(CONT STEIN)

O I see, so you knew him very well?

(asked he, serious?) (LOOKING AT HIM)

(CONT REYNOLDS)

(Excuse me, said her walking over to AIL)

(CONT REYNOLDS)

AIL, do you have a time of death yet?

(asked her, seriously?) (LOOKING AT HIM)

(AIL stood up, holding L.B. wallet in his hand, LOOKING AT HER.)

(CONT AIL)

MICHELLE, according to his body, temperature and lost of blood, sometime after 1'AM this morning. (He open the wallet) His name is LUTHER BRASWELL. he live right here. I'll tell you something else MICHELLE. (AIL looking at the body) who ever this vigilant murdering person is, this man knew his assassin(LOOKING AT HER) he took two in the chest no more then three feet away. my question is what did he do (MEANING L.B.) for someone to do such a thing like this?

(Nodded no, said he, a serious face.) (LOOKING AT HER)

(CONT REYNOLDS)

AIL, I have no answer yet because of these killings. But I promise you this(Nodded yes) I will not stop, I will not rest until I get or find some sort of meaningful closure behind all of this killings. If we catch this person or person or not. even if I just simply end up killing this vigilant murdering damn S.O.B. myself, (said her. a little loud irritated.) (LOOKING AT HIM)

(DIALOGUE)

(STEIN, notice TYLER on the other side of the fence, in his yard, LOOKING AT THEM)

(CONT STEIN)

Mr. PATTERSON, who's that guy over there. (He pointed to TYLER.)

(asked he, direct face?) (LOOKING AT HIM)

(CONT KEVIN)

I don't know him personal. (He LOOK'S AT TYLER) all I know is, he live there.

(Nodded yes, answer he.) (LOOKING AT STEIN)

(DIALOGUE)

(STEIN walked over to TYLER. He showed his badge)

(CONT STEIN)

Sir, my name is detective STEIN. What is your name sir?

(asked he serious?) (LOOKING AT TYLER)

(TYLER)

Detective my name is TYLER NELSON. Detective is L.B. dead?)

(said and asked he, expression of respect.) (LOOKING AT STEIN

(CONT STEIN)

Mr. NELSON about how well did you know him. The one you call L.B. (he pointed to L.B.)

(asked he, serious?) (LOOKING AT TYLER.)

(CONT TYLER)

Detective, I knew him well enough to stay away from his property line, especial when he turn his mean ass dog's out into his yard. sometime on the week-end, he may have some sort of activity going on, concerning all the traffic coming and going. the guy you were just talking to I see him a lot of time's there with other people. and sometime's his girlfriend. I think her name is DIANE or something.

(answer he, direct face.) (LOOKING AT HIM.)

(CONT STEIN)

Did you notice any special activity or lot's of traffic last night?

(asked he, seriously?) (LOOKING AT HIM)

(CONT TYLER)

(Nodded no) No, you know detective, it were unusual real quite (A STUN LOOK) around here last night. (Nodded yes) normally about twice a month, L.B will have at least something like a party were going on with all the traffic and activity of people going in and out of his house, on the week-end.

(said he, seriously.) (LOOKING AT STEIN)

(CONT STEIN)

Would there be any trouble among any of these people that you notice or witness going in and out of there?

(asked he sincere?) (LOOKING AT HIM)

(CONT TYLER)

Detective, I'm sure if there were any trouble going on, that guy you were talking to(HE LOOKED AT KEVIN) he should know, (answer he, seriously.) (LOOKING AT STEIN)

(CONT STEIN)

O yeah, thanks' a lot sir.

(said he, (LOOKING AT KEVIN STANDING IN THE DRIVEWAY, WALKING OVER TO REYNOLDS.)

(CONT STEIN)

MICHELLE, I was just inform by that guy standing on the other side of that fence(Nodded toward TYLER)

(CONT STEIN)

That guy standing in the driveway,(Nodded toward KEVIN) be here a lot with other people on the week-end, like decrease were having a party or something. (said he, seriously.) (LOOKING AT HER)

(DIALOGUE)

(Come on STEVE, let's have a talk with Mr. PATTERSON, said her as they were walking over to KEVIN.)

(CONT STEIN)

Mr. PATTERSON, we would like to ask you some question sir, if you do not mine? (asked he sincere?) (Nodded yes, LOOKING AT HIM)

(CONT KEVIN)

No I don't mine, go a head, (answer he respectfully.) (LOOKING AT THEM)

(CONT REYNOLDS)

Where were you last night sir, Let's say around 1'AM? (asked her sincere?) (LOOKING AT KEVIN)

(CONT KEVIN)

Detective, after I got off work, I went home where I live with my parents. I did not leave until it were time for me to take L.B to his car dealer ship this morning. (said he, straight face.) (LOOKING AT THEM)

(CONT REYNOLDS)

Where do you work and live sir? and what time did you leave work sir?

(CONT REYNOLDS)

(asked her seriously?) (LOOKING AT HIM)

(CONT KEVIN)

I work's at walmart warehouse, over on evergreen LN. I live on Ashley CT. I clocked out at midnight last night and I went straight home. My job and my parents can verify that, (said he respectfully.) (LOOKING AT THEM)

(CONT STEIN)

(Nodded yes) 0 I see, do you know if Mr. BRASWELL had any enemy's or if anyone made any serious threat's against him lately? (asked he, direct face?) (LOOKING AT KEVIN)

(CONT KEVIN)

(Nodded no) Detective, I have never witness or heard L.B, getting into an argument with no one, that I can think of, L.B.

were well liked by every body. (Nodded yes) if he had an enemy I sure hell don't know who that person would be. (said he, honestly.) (LOOKING AT THEM)

(DIALOGUE)

(REYNOLDS notice officer's PETE and ROY at the end of the driveway talking near the street. She walked over to them.)

(CONT REYNOLDS)

Morning PETE, morning ROY. (said her, serious.) (LOOKING AT THEM.)

(BOTH OFFICER"S)

Morning detective,
(answer them.) (LOOKING AT HER)

(CONT REYNOLDS)

Have yall found out anything yet from canvassing the area? (asked her, direct serious serious?) (LOOKING AT THEM)

(PETE)

Detective,(Nodded no) we having found any evidence or any witness at all concerning this crime, (said he seriously.) (LOOKING AT HER)

(ROY)

It seems detective, who ever this murdering person is, he or she, really do know how to clean up their evidence real good. I mean there are no shell casing no foot print's, or any D.N.A, to be found. This were a real clean professional hit here, (said he frustrate.) (LOOKING AT HER)

(CONT REYNOLDS)

I know ROY,(Nodded yes) calm down, this one here is a real careful one. That's why I'm so determine to catch this one, or if necessary kill, (said her, with passion.) (LOOKING AT THEM)

(CONT PETE)

Detective, do you think it will come to something like that? (asked he, nodded head,) (PUTTING ONE HAND ON HER SHOULDER)

(CONT REYNOLDS)

This is a real smart one here PETE. Nothing will surprise me about this person reaction when we catch he or she, responsible for all these killings, (said her with affection.) (LOOKING AT PETE)

(DIALOGUE)

(STEIN walked over to MICHELLE, and the two officer's, while AIL, and another forensic guy were preparing L.B, body for transporting it to forensic EMILY office for Autopsy.)

(CONT REYNOLDS)

Thanks' a lot PETE and ROY. If you do fine something, let me know at once, (said her, serious.) (LOOKING AT THEM)

(DIALOGUE)

As REYNOLDS and STEIN enter their car to leave the scene, with STEIN driving.

(CONT STEIN)

MICHELLE, when we get back to the station, I think I'm going to run a back ground check on Mr. BRASWELL. And see if I can fine anything on him important or negligence on his behalf. Because PATTERSON, sound like Mr. BRASWELL was one of the good guy's in his neighbor hood, never no wrong doing on his part. (said he, professional innocent.)

(CONT REYNOLDS)

Just what are you expect to fine on this man STEVE? (asked her, direct?) (LOOKING AT HIM)

(CONT STEIN)

MICHELLE, if you do not mind, let's get back to the station first please, and fine out, please.

(answer he, serious.) (DRIVING)

(DIALOGUE)

After STEVE and MICHELLE, returned to the police station. STEIN begins running a back ground check on LUTHER BRASWELL. He found out that LUTHER had recently been arrested and released for narcotic and hiding huge amount of cash from the I.R.S. and he had been dealing in narcotic for a very long period of time.

NEW-SCENE (DIALOGUE)

SLUG-LINE-THE-NEXT-WEEK

LIEUTENANT-SCOTT-MACK-OFFICE

TUESDAY-EVENING

That Monday doing lunch break at the court house, assistant D.A. JAMES FUTCH heard about Mr. LUTHER BRASWELL assassination that pass week-end before from officer PETE in the hallway. So that Tuesday, after court, FUTCH decided he would pay Mr. SCOTT MACK a visit at his office. on his arrival there he knocked on the door. SCOTT talking on the phone.

(SCOTT)

Come in. (said he.)

(FUTCH enter in and closed the door behind him, SCOTT stood up and hang up the phone.)

(JAMES)

SCOTT, I hope you are not real business, I need to talk to you, if you don't mind? (said and asked he serious?) (LOOKING AT HIM)

(CONT SCOTT)

No JAMES, I don't mine, have a seat, what is this all about? (answer and asked he, serious?) (LOOKING AT HIM)

(CONT FUTCH)

SCOTT, I have a serious hunch, base on judge SAM MASON attitude toward any defendant, that stand's before him, just for arrangement, whatever the disturbing charger's maybe. I can request for a high ball, but judge MASON would give them a lower bail and somehow within a few day's or week's they turn up shot to death dead man. (said he straight face.) (LOOKING AT HIM)

(CONT SCOTT)

JAMES, are you telling me, that judge MASON have something to do with these killing's. (A SERIOUS LOOK) come on JAMES, you got to do better then that. (NODDED NO) that nice old man don't have the heart or the nerve to do something like that.

(said he, very surprise face.) (LOOKING AT HIM)

(CONT FUTCH)

SCOTT, you may not believe me, but something is very much going on. If he is not doing it his self then he must know the thug who is responsible, or he maybe having a thug doing for him. (said he, honest attitude.) (LOOKING AT HIM)

(CONT SCOTT)

(NODDED NO) JAMES, have you lost your damn mind man. The start with, I don't appreciate this shit man. Do you have proof at all something like that has been happening here man. Let me tell you something, if you planning to go after judge MASON with these allegation with no proof, you just go right head. and you can just count me out, I mean that man. (said he, a little loud.) (LOOKING AT JAMES)

(CONT FUTCH)

SCOTT, will you just wait a damn minute, you tell me why the last seven defendant stood before judge MASON, just for a arrangement turn up dead, in just a few damn day's or week's. I serious believe judge MASON is involve some way, some how with these motherfucking killing's, (said he, strong voice.) (LOOKING AT SCOTT)

(CONT SCOTT)

JAMES, I know you and judge MASON have had yall different in the pass man. But I personally think you are making a very stupid crazy mistake here. (A STRAIGHT FACE) JAMES if you want to make these allegation of your own freewill, you go right head and commit suicide on your damn own. MICHELLE and STEVE

(CONT SCOTT)

are working hard to find the S.O.B. responsible for these damn killing's. They need time man, can't you see that. (said he, a little angry.) (LOOKING AT HIM)

(CONT FUTCH)

(NODDED NO FRUSTRATION FACE) O SCOTT,(EXCITED) let me talk to MICHELLE and STEVE about this. They may have found some evidence or they may have a suspect in mind. if not, will you please man, Let them check into it.

I don't think it will hurt anyone come on SCOTT, just let me talk to them in your presence man. That's all I'm asking you for right now, please, (said he, straight face.) (LOOKING AT SCOTT)

(CONT SCOTT)

(NODDED NO) I don't know JAMES, how soon you want to talk to them about a impossible stupid crazy thing like this. But I'm warning you JAMES, I will not allow them to take any blame behind this stupid crazy idea of yours man. I mean that.

(NODDED YES) Do you understand me JAMES.

(said he, strong voice.) (LOOKING AT HIM)

(CONT FUTCH)

Yes I understand SCOTT. Can you call them in right now SCOTT? (asked he, serous?) (LOOKING AT HIM)

(CONT SCOTT)

(SHAKING HEAD NO) No, I will not, Let me talk to them first. Believe me JAMES, they have their hands full now investigating these damn killing's, Ok.

(A brisk look, said he.) (LOOKING AT HIM)

(CONT)

(THEY STOOD UP)

(CONT FUTCH)

Alright SCOTT, that's fare enough for right now. But let me know as soon as you can. alright sir? (said he, sincere.) (LOOKING AT SCOTT)

(FUTCH started to walk out)

(CONT SCOTT)

JAMES, I'll give you a call sometime tomorrow evening after court. (said he, straight face.) (LOOKING AT HIM)

(DIALOGUE)

(FUTCH, wave his hand and leave's SCOTT office.) The next day, SCOTT call FUTCH office and left word for him to be at his office around five O'clock that Wednesday, evening. FUTCH arrived on time. They are all sitting down, in SCOTT office.

(SCOTT)

JAMES, I have already brief MICHELLE and STEVE about your, Theory and idea. They are willing to listening to what you have to say OK. (said he, serious.) (LOOKING AT HIM)

(MICHELLE and STEVE look's at JAMES.)

(FUTCH)

Let me first thank you-all for allowing me to express my Theory, of what I think have been happening. When hard

(CONT FUTCH)

cold criminal stand's before judge MASON for their arrangement, what ever bail I ask for, judge MASON always give that criminal a lower bail. After he or she post that bail with in a few day's or week's some how they turn up shot to death. My theory is I think judge MASON is involve some how. Now my question to you-all. Would you be willing to look into my theory, (said and asked he, very seriously?) (LOOKING AT THEM)

(MICHELLE, look's at SCOTT) surprise face

(REYNOLDS)

Lieutenant, have Mr. FUTCH lost his mind. Mr. FUTCH do you have any thread of evidence, judge MASON is involve with people being kill? (said and asked her; respectfully?) (LOOKING AT JAMES)

(STEIN)

Mr. FUTCH, how did you come to such theory? (asked he a little loud?) (LOOKING AT JAMES)

(CONT FUTCH)

(NODDED YES) I know you-all have been investigating several murder's lately. But I sure you everyone of those people stood before judge MASON and received a very low bail, the next thing we know they are dead, (said he, irritated.) (LOOKING AT THEM)

(CONT REYNOLDS)

So Mr. FUTCH, you are expecting STEVE and I to give up our career, because of your stupid absent mind theory with no proof.

(said and asked her, a little loud.?) (LOOKING AT JAMES)

(CONT FUTCH)

Alright, do you have any suspect at this point and time? (asked he, a little frustrate?) (LOOKING AT THEM)

(CONT STEIN)

Mr. FUTCH, Let me ask you a question? How long have you been living insane man? Going after judge MASON, is not of our favor thing's with no proof, (asked and said he, excited?) (LOOKING AT JAMES)

(MICHELLE look's at SCOTT)

(CONT REYNOLDS)

Lieutenant, what do you think of this? (asked her irritated?) (LOOKING AT SCOTT)

(CONT SCOTT)

I really can't see how anyone can look into something like this, with out judge MASON knowing about it.

(said he, with a since of human,) (LOOKING AT THEM)

(CONT FUTCH)

Well SCOTT, I were always told, if there is will, then there is a way. We will just have to find away, with out judge MASON knowing anything about, (said he, very irritated.) (LOOKING AT SCOTT)

(DIALOGUE)

(Just as SCOTT started to speak, STEIN snapped his finger.)

(CONT STEIN)

Lieutenant, I just may have a way, without judge MASON ever knowing anything at all about this. Only if Mr. FUTCH theory is correct and accurate about judge MASON involvement, with these killing's, (said he, sincere.) (LOOKING AT SCOTT)

(CONT SCOTT)

Just what are you getting at STEVE? Let me tell yall something. It is true we all deserve to know the true on this thing. But if this situation slip out of our hand's at all. and judge MASON find's out what we are doing. What do you-all thinks' will happen to us all? Do we all understands each other about this? (said and asked he? straight face) (LOOKING AT THEM)

(THEY ALL NODDED YES AND SAID YES)

(CONT SCOTT)

Good, now let me hear what you have to say STEVE.
(said he.)

(FUTCH and MICHELLE looking and listening at STEVE)

(CONT STEIN)

Lieutenant, I think I know away, I have a friend, I think I can get him to play a dumb charge right in front of judge MASON. and see if judge will give him a lower bond to get out of jail. And who ever comes after him in two or three day's or week's, we will be right in place to catch him or she.

(said he, sensitive.) (LOOKING AT SCOTT)

(CONT SCOTT)

STEVE, all that sound good, but how do we know this person can be trusted. before, doing, and after we catch who ever? (said and asked he, straight face?) (LOOKING AT STEVE)

(CONT STEIN)

Lieutenant,(NODDED YES) You can trust me on this one. his name is JACOB WILLIAMS. I've been knowing him sense junior high school. He is about my height and age. he is an African American. lieutenant, I sure you. you will never meet a very intelligent smart man, like he is. I think J.W. is the best opportunity we have to catch the judge or whoever responsible for these murder's.

(said he, professional.) (LOOKING AT SCOTT)

(CONT REYNOLDS)

STEVE, you are that sure, of this guy? (asked her, normally?) (LOOKING AT STEVE)

(CONT STEIN)

Yes MICHELLE, I'm very sure about J.W. (Nodded yes, answer he.) (LOOKING AT HER)

(CONT SCOTT)

Well JAMES, what do you think of STEVE theory? (asked he, serious?) (LOOKING AT JAMES)

(CONT FUTCH)

SCOTT, if no one here talk's about it to no one, I think it will work. Because I know judge MASON, he is involve some how, and some way. and if we catch this person, trust me, I will make he or she talk, so we will know the true

(CONT FUTCH)

thug murdering S.O.B. killing people, like they have their own secret justice going on. it is not right in our society while some people are setting around playing grab ass with each other, while some S.O.B. killing innocent people for no damn reason. (said he, a little angry.) (LOOKING AT SCOTT)

(CONT SCOTT)

STEVE, how soon are you planning to talk to this person. As you can see, JAMES here he's all for it. No matter what the hell we think, (said he honestly.) (LOOKING AT STEVE.)

(CONT STEIN)

I'LL stop by his place tomorrow and see if I can get thing's set up with him. (HE LOOK"S AT FUTCH) Mr. FUTCH after I get it set up, I'll contact lieutenant here, and he will contact you. if that's alright with you sir? (said and asked he, serious?) (LOOKING AT JAMES)

(CONT FUTCH)

That sound good to me. (Nodded yes, answer he.) (LOOKING AT STEVE)

(CONT SCOTT)

Alright, this conversation never leave's this office until I say so. That also go's for you to JAMES, (said he straight face.) (LOOKING AT ALL OF THEM.)

(DIALOGUE)

(They all agreed and walked out.)

NEW-SCENE-

(DIALOGUE)

EXT-INT-JACOB WILLIAMS-HOUSE

THURSDAY-EVENING-6'PM-EMILY-AUTOPSY-OFFICE

MICHELLE, went to see EMILY about L.B. autopsy, STEVE went to have a talk with J.W.

On MICHELLE, arrival into EMILY office,. EMILY and AIL were standing in her office talking

(REYNOLDS)

Hello EMILY, Hello AIL. (said her, a little smile.) (LOOKING AT THEM)

(EMILY, AIL)

Hello MICHELLE, (answer them Both.) (LOOKING AT HER)

(CONT MICHELLE)

EMILY, can we talk for a few minute's? (asked her sincere?) (LOOKING AT EMILY)

(CONT EMILY)

(NODDEDYESANDSAIDYES) ExcuseusAIL. (WALKING AWAY) (AIL WALKED OUT THE OFFICE) MICHELLE, you sound so sincere, like this is a private conversation, (said her seriously.) (LOOKING AT MICHELLE.)

(CONT REYNOLDS)

EMILY, if you do not mind, I need some serious straight answer about Mr. BRASWELL autopsy. like what kind of weapon was used on this man. (said her sincere?) (LOOKING AT HER)

(DIALOGUE)
(EMILY walked to her desk and picked up a file)

(CONT EMILY)
MICHELLE, I'm absolute sure Mr. BRASWELL were kill with a 9mm gun. After talking to TERSA, according to her, the same 9mm gun kill several other people recently. she said Ballistics matched right up(She clear her throat a little) MICHELLE, in Mr. BRASWELL case this man had enough toxicate chemical in his body, such as cocaine and alcohol, that will knock an elephant down or knock a shark out the ocean. MICHELLE this man was so intoxicate, he never knew that he had been shot, with all that cocaine and alcohol in his blood. (She licked her lip's) MICHELLE, why do you seems so uncomfortable about Mr. BRASWELL death? (said and asked her sincere?) (LOOKING AT HER)

(CONT REYNOLDS)
EMILY, there maybe something going on I can not discuss with you at this time and point. But thank you EMILY for that report. (NODDED YES)
(said her, sincere.) (LOOKING AT EMILY)

(MICHELLE WALKED OUT)

(DIALOGUE)
After climbing the step's on to the front porch, at J.W. house. STEVE knocked on the front door, with J.W to answer it

(JW)
Well, hello STEVE, COME ON in. (said he smiling.) (LOOKING AT STEVE)

(DIALOGUE) (STEVE enter the house, as they are shaking hands)

(STEIN)
Hello your self J.W. (answer he, smiling) (LOOKING AT HIM)

(CONT J.W.)
Have a seat. (THEY SIT DOWN IN THE LIVINGROOM) It's been a while since I seen you STEVE, now what brings you by here? (said and asked he?) (LOOKING AT HIM)

(CONT STEIN)
Well, J.W, I need to talk to you about something, if you don't mind? (said and asked he, stun look?) (LOOKING AT J.W.)

(CONT J.W.)
STEVE, why do you sound so sincere? (asked he serious?) (LOOKING AT STEVE)

(CONT STEIN)
(Clear his throat) Because J.W. I have a situation at work no one is sure of what they think is happen or really happen. (said he seriously.) (LOOKING AT HIM)

(CONT J.W.)
Just what are you talking about STEVE? (asked he seriously?) (LOOKING AT HIM)

(CONT STEIN)
J.W. I never forgetting about that play you were in, back in school, and you were very good with the character you played, (said he, seriously.) (LOOKING AT HIM)

(CONT J.W.)

STEVE, just what in the hell, a school play has to do with your job and me?

(said and asked he, serious?) (LOOKING AT HIM)

(CONT STEIN)

J.W. I'm sure by now, you problem have heard from the news media or the news paper about several killings in our county. And there has never been any arrest on these murder's, (said he serious?) (LOOKING AT J.W.)

(CONT J.W.)

(NODDED YES) O yeah, yes I have heard STEVE, But what's that got to do with me. I hope you are not making me a suspect in these murder's? (asked he, seriously?) (LOOKING AT STEVE)

(CONT STEIN)

(NODDED NO) No J.W. There are people I can not name at this point an time. They seem to think that someone who ever it is, work's at the court house responsible or behind these damn killing's. do you understand J.W.? (said and asked he, very concern?) (LOOKING AT HIM)

(CONT J.W.)

So STEVE, just what do you think I can do about it? (asked he, straight face?) (LOOKING AT HIM)

(CONT STEIN)

You see J.W. I have an idea, I think it just may work to catch who ever responsible for these murder's. I was hoping I could trust you to play a dummy murder charge in front of one judge.

(STEVE SET UP STRAIGHT)

Now J.W. please just hear me out. (J.W. LOOKED STRAIGHT AT HIM) There is a judge normally he give's the low's bail doing any arrangement and after these people post bail and get out of jail with in two or three day's or week's. someone in the court house or the court room, either they send someone or they are doing it them self to kill these people. Now I promise you J.W. you will be safe at all time, you will be protected, and you will not be hurt in no way at all. and you will be reburst of any money's you may spend. I promise you J.W. (said he straight serious face.) (LOOKING AT J.W.)

(CONT J.W.)

(REAL EXCITED) STEVE, you mean to tell me, you want me to just lay down my life for you and the damn entire police force, just like that, so you-all can try and catch a mother fucking murder, you think is murdering people, STEVE, I do have a sense of pride about myself man. (said he seriously.) (LOOKING AT STEVE)

(J.W stood up as STEVE, started to walk out)

(CONT STEIN)

J.W. I did not mean you any harm. it justed I thought I would ask a friend to help a friend to catch a murder, that's all man, I'm sorry if I invade your privacy.

(HE NODDED) again I'm sorry man. (said he, very sensitive.) (LOOKING AT J.W.)

(CONT J.W.)

STEVE, I'm sorry too. By the way STEVE, do you still have that fine sister as your partner? (asked he? a little smile?) (LOOKING AT HIM)

(CONT STEIN)

(NODDED YES SMILE) 0 yeah, MICHELLE is still my partner, and if you decide to help us out, she will be there protecting you as well. (said he, a little excited.) (LOOKING AT J.W.

(CONT J.W.)

STEVE, let me think about this, I'LL Let you know something in a day are so. (SMILING) you have a real fine sister working with you my friend, (said he, rubbing his hair.) (LOOKING AT STEVE)

(STEVE looked at J.W. and walked on out.)

(DIALOGUE)

Three day's pass and J.W. decided he would help his friend STEVE out. After notifying STEVE of his decision by phone. STEVE contacted lieutenant SCOTT MACK.

NEW-SCENE (DIALOGUE)

SLUG-LINE-ONE-MONTH-LATER

COURT-ROOM-ARRANGEMENT-MONDAY-MORNING

CHARACTER-JUDGE-SAM MASON

CHARACTER-ASSISTANT-D.A.-JAMES FUTCH

CHARACTER-JACOB WILLIAMS

CHARACTER-ATTORNEY-DONALD OLIVE

COURT ROOM FULL OF PEOPLE

(MONICA)

Your honor, docket number 02310 the state verse one Mr. JACOB WILLIAMS. The charge is murder in the first degree, (said her, normal voice.) (LOOKING AT JUDGE MASON, AS SHE HANDED HIM THE PAPER WORK.)

(JUDGE MASON SEATED IN HIS CHAIR)
Mr. OLIVE, with all due respect, how do your client plead? (asked he, serious?) (LOOKING AT HIM)

(MR. OLIVE STANDING WITH J.W.)
Your honor, with the appreciation of the court not guilty your honor, (answer he straight face.) (LOOKING AT THE JUDGE)

(CONT JUDGE)
Thank you sir.
(answer he seriously,)
(JUDGE MASON LOOKED AT MR. FUTCH)

(CONT JUDGE)

Mr. FUTCH, may I please have Application for bail sir?
(asked he, attitude?) (LOOKING AT HIM)

(FUTCH STANDING)
Your honor, with out any presidential or any argument The state is requesting two hundred fifty thousand dollars, on bail sir. (said he, respectful.) (LOOKING AT THE JUDGE)

(CONT JUDGE)
(A VERY STUN LOOK) That's all? you'll not going to ask for more, or give me a hard time, this time? (asked he, surprise?) (LOOKING AT FUTCH)

(CONT FUTCH)

(NODDED NO) No your honor.
(answer he.) (LOOKING AT THE JUDGE)

(CONT JUDGE)

Well, if that's the case, Mr. WILLIAMS, you are here by order not to leave orange county or the state of north Carolina until trial. Bail is set at ten thousand dollars, cash or bond., next case. (HE TAP HIS GAVEL) (said he, straight face.) (LOOKING AT FUTCH AND J.W.)

(DIALOGUE)

(They all nodded yes, and walked out of court. J.W. posted bail that morning and were released from jail.)

NEW-SCENE

(DIALOGUE)
SLUG-LINE-EARLY-SATURDAY-MORNING-OF-THAT-WEEK-2 AM
J.W.-APARTMENT-CHAPEL-HILL-
NC-ON-MISTY-RUN-CT

By J.W. played a dummy charge in court, he also had a dummy address on misty run CT. So this is what happen early that Saturday morning.

The apartment complex had a driveway in the back and out front or you could park on the street, out front.

MICHELLE, lieutenant MACK, and FUTCH were parked out back in a van with dark window's. STEIN and officer PETE were parked out front in a van, with dark window's on the street. Suddenly a black Mercedes pull in back of the apartment, light's off. A second black Mercedes pull in front, light's off. Secret justice in both car's. Put on black glove's, screw silence on barrel of 9mm gun's, put black ski mass over head's, exit out of car, real quietly with gun's in hand's, started walking up to apartment slow, looking around, as they walked toward the apartment, very fast MICHELLE, and lieutenant MACK jumped out of van. Hold it there)said he loud.) (LOOKING AT SECRET JUSTICE.) secret justice stop's and turned around. STEIN and

PETE got out of their van quietly behind secret justice,(STEIN Hold it there) (said he loud) secret justice stop's and turned around. Both secret justice, raised their arm's with gun's pointed to shoot, MICHELLE fired two shot's, killing secret justice, instantly, STEIN and PETE fired twice killing secret justice out front instantly. J.W. exit out of his apartment instantly in shock out front. MICHELLE and MACK walked over to the body, FUTCH get's out of van, and walked to them. MICHELLE bended down, and removed ski mass from the dead person head. They looked at each other in total shock

(CONT DIALOGUE)

It turned out to be transcript recorder MARTHA JONES. After STEIN removed ski mass from dead person out front, STEIN and PETE looked at each other in total shock. It turned out to be sheriff GEORGE BLUE. STEIN walked behind the apartment, leaving PETE and J.W. out front.

(STEIN)

Lieutenant, MICHELLE, what are you'll shooting at? we got the shooter around front, (said he, serious, pointing his thumb back(LOOKING AT THEM)

(SCOTT)

STEVE, look who this is, you want believe it. (said he, serious) (LOOKING AT STEVE)

STEVE, bended down and looked at the body)

(CONT STEIN)

Lieutenant, that's MARTHA JONES, from court, (said he, sincere.) (LOOKING AT THEM)

(REYNOLDS)

STEVE, just who were yall shooting at around front? (asked her, sincere?) (LOOKING AT HIM)

(CONT STEIN)

You-all want believe it. Please go take a look who that shooter is. (said he.) (LOOKING AT THEM)

(DIALOGUE)

(CONT DIALOGUE)

They all walked around front to see the dead body,. MICHELLE had MARTHA. 9mm gun in a plastic bag. PETE had the sheriff 9mm gun in a plastic bag.

(FUTCH)

You see SCOTT, I was right. I knew someone in the court or at the court house was involve with these damn killing's. These two here, are in judge MASON court room every day. listening to what is sayed and done in there. Now my question now is. Just what the hell that S.O.B. judge MASON know about this, or these two here, (said he, angry.) (LOOKING AT SCOTT)

(CONT SCOTT)

JAMES, I can see your theory were right. But we still don't have any proof or evidence judge MASON is involve with these damn killing's man. (said he, angry.) (LOOKING AT FUTCH)

(CONT FUTCH)

Well SCOTT, I have a surprise for you. I personal checked judge MASON outs and I found out he also own a 9mm gun. and right now, I think we need to go to his house and run his gun through ballistics. And SCOTT, I'm willing to bets we will not" be surprise about his involvement in these damn killing's either, (said he, sincere.) (LOOKING AT HIM)

(CONT SCOTT)

That maybe true JAMES. But right now, we don't have a warrant or a court order to go to his house this time of morning

(CONT SCOTT)

looking for nothing either, (said he concern.) (LOOKING AT HIM)

(CONT FUTCH)

Well, when the sun come up, I guarantee you, I will have that court order,

(said he, straight face.) (LOOKING AT HIM)

(CONT SCOTT)

That's fine with me JAMES. But myself, MICHELLE, and STEVE, we are coming with you, if you like it or not. (said he, straight face.) (LOOKING AT HIM)

(CONT FUTCH)

Fine SCOTT. (said he.) (LOOKING AT ALL of THEM)

(CONT SCOTT)

PETE get these gun's to ballistics right now. MICHELLE you or STEVE one, get AIL out here to take care of these body's,

(SCOTT LOOKED AT J.W.)

(CONT SCOTT)

Mr. WILLIAMS, you did very good, thanks' you very kindly for helping us out sir.

(said he, polite. (SHAKING HIS HAND, LOOKING AT HIM)

(J.W.)

Lieutenant, if there's someone else out here running around with a gun killing people. I sure hell don't want to be his next victim, yall be sure and get that S.O.B. real fast too

(said he sincere.) (LOOKING AT MICHELLE, SMILING)

(DIALOGUE)

After AIL arrived with another forensic guy to remove the two body's. They all(left the scene until the sun came up

NEW-SCENE-

(DIALOGUE)

SLUG-LINE-JUDGE-MASON-HOUSE-CHAPEL-HILL-NC-FOXRIDGE RD
CHARACTER-WIFE-ESTER MASON-7:30 AM-THAT-MORNING

After lieutenant Mack, FUTCH, MICHELLE and STEVE pulled in front of judge MASON house, they all exited out of their car's, and walked up the step's to front door. SCOTT rang the door bell!, with Mrs. ESTER MASON to answer it, in her pajama and bath robe. (THE DOOR OPEN)

(ESTER)

Good morning, can I help you-all with something?
(said and asked her, concern look.) (LOOKING AT THEM)

(SCOTT, HE SHOWED HIS BADGE)

Mam, I'm lieutenant SCOTT MACK, this is ADA, JAMES FUTCH,—and these are detective REYNOLDS and STEIN. Mam, is judge MASON here (said and asked he polite?) (LOOKING AT HER)

(CONT ESTER)

Yes he is here, wait just minute,(NODDED YES) I'LL get him for you. (answer her, polite) (AS SHE TURNED AROUND, WALKING DOWN THE HALL
(JUDGE MASON CAME UP FRONT OUT FROM HIS STUDY IN HIS PAJAMA AND BATH ROBE)

(CONT JUDGE)

Just what the hell, you people want this time of morning? (asked he? attitude) (LOOKING AT THEM)

(CONT SCOTT)

Sorry to disturb you this time of morning sir, But do you own a 9mm gun sir?

(asked he, polite) (LOOKING AT HIM)

(CONT JUDGE)

Yes why? (answer he. strong voice.) (LOOKING AT THEM)

(CONT SCOTT)

Judge, I have a court order signed here, by judge RAYMOND BURNS, to take your gun for ballistics sir. (said he, polite.) (LOOKING AT HIM)

(CONT JUDGE)

Ballistics, just what in the hell for? (asked he? angry) (LOOKING AT THEM)

(REYNOLDS)

Judge, we don't want any trouble sir? just give us the gun sir. (said her polite.) (LOOKING AT HIM)

(FUTCH)

Unless, you have something to hide sir? (said he, angry attitude.) (LOOKING AT HIM)

(CONT JUDGE)

Alright, it's in my study, I'll get it for you I'll be right back.

(DIALOGUE)

As judge MASON turned around walking down the hall, going toward his study. They all enter the house behind him. When the judge enter his study, he closed the door behind him. Suddenly they all heard a very loud gunshot, where they all rushed down the hall into the judge study and found judge SAM MASON dead, from committed suicide in his chair.

THE END . . . FADE OUT